OPERATOR 5:
DRUMS OF DESTRUCTION

SECRET SERVICE #5 ™
OPERATOR 5
AMERICA'S UNDERCOVER ACE

DRUMS OF
DESTRUCTION

By Curtis Steele

POPULAR PUBLICATIONS • 2022

CHAPTER 1
OPERATOR 5'S MESSENGERS

THE STEEL-HELMETED Uhlans were everywhere. For the third time that morning, the two riders were compelled to spur their horses off the highway and into the tall wheat in the adjoining fields, in order to avoid the Uhlan patrols.

Twenty men and a sergeant—each patrol was the same in number. And on the helmets of those troopers was emblazoned the same grisly insignia—the symbol of the crossed broadswords and the severed head, under which these troops of the Purple Empire had conquered two-thirds of the world.

The two riders stood motionless in the wheat beside their horses, hands close to their holstered guns, prepared to sell their lives dearly if they should be discovered.

One of these two was a beautiful, chestnut-haired young woman whose trim figure was not entirely concealed by the khaki riding breeches and uniform blouse she wore; the other was hardly more than a boy—somewhere between fifteen and sixteen, freckle-faced, pert-nosed. There was no fear in the eyes of either—only a tense wariness combined with the sparkle of great daring.

The earth was soft under their feet where they stood, with the wheat growing about them, for it had rained all night. They

1

could distinctly hear the clatter of the hooves of the Uhlans' mounts as the patrol spurred westward along the highway.

The boy leaned over past his horse's head, and whispered to the young woman: "Gosh, Diane, there must be something doing. These patrols are thick as flies!"

The young woman nodded somberly. "They're probably watching every road west. Marshal Kremer is no fool. He knows that our men will be hurrying to join the American Defense Force now, and he wants to head them off, Tim."

Tim grinned tightly. "There are plenty of roads out here that Kremer and his troops don't know anything about. The boys'll be able to get by all right. And even if they do meet a patrol—I feel sorry for the patrol!"

Oregon bayonets flashed
down into the trench.

"I hope you're right," Diane said fervently. Abruptly, she gripped the boy's arm. "Look, Tim! The patrol is stopping! If they've discovered us—"

"No, no, Di. It's not us. See, they're looking over toward that shack on the other side of the road!"

It was true. The Purple sergeant was issuing orders, and now Diane and Tim saw two of the Uhlans spurring across the opposite field toward a small tumbledown shack some two hundred yards off the road.

"I hope they finish their poking around quick!" Tim said fiercely. "We've got work to do, and we can't hide here all day!"

The patrol sat stiffly on their restive horses, while the two troopers dismounted in front of the shack, and one of them struck loudly against the door with the butt of his rifle. "Open up within!" he shouted, in the language of the Purple Empire.

There was no answer from inside the shack.

Diane and Tim watched, holding their breath. They saw the burly sergeant in the road wave impatiently. "Break down the door!" he shouted. "And be quick!"

The troopers obeyed. Their rifle butts smashed again and again at the flimsy door, and it swung inward. The two troopers disappeared inside.

Suddenly, a shriek sounded from the interior of the shack.

Diane gasped. "Tim! They've caught somebody there!"

The shriek was repeated twice, then was suddenly stilled. Tim scowled, and put a hand on his gun. "Damn them! That's a woman's voice—"

He broke off, staring narrow-eyed through the wheat.

4

DRUMS OF DESTRUCTION

THE TWO troopers were emerging from the shack. One of them was dragging a woman by the hair. The second was yanking two small children, one by each arm. They were a boy and a girl, the boy about five, the girl about seven. The two children were too frightened to resist, but their mother fought frantically with the trooper, trying to cling to the youngsters. The trooper retained his grip on her hair, laughing brutally. He snatched up the reins of his horse, and, followed by the second trooper dragging the two children, made his way back to the road.

The wretched woman stumbled after him, moaning with the agony of the merciless grip on her hair.

In the road, the two troopers let go of their three captives, and mounted their horses again. Immediately the mother ran to the boy and girl, threw her arms around them, pressing them to her breast.

Diane and Tim, watching from their hiding place in the wheat fields, sighed with relief. Tim said: "They're going to leave them alone, Di. Look, the sergeant is only going to question them."

The sergeant of Uhlans rode his horse close to the woman, growled down at her: "What is your name, woman?"

"Anna Mooney," she told him, looking up fearfully.

"Where is your husband?"

"He—he isn't here."

The sergeant laughed shortly. "Probably gone to join the American army, eh?"

Anna Mooney did not answer. Her two children cowered close to her, staring wide-eyed at the burly troopers.

The two watchers in the wheat field had heard her answer clearly. Tim whispered to Diane: "That's John Mooney's wife—the man we're supposed to meet! If those Uhlans guess that her husband is planning to lead a battalion of Americans to join the Defense Force, they'd shoot her on the spot!"

"Let's pray they don't know it!" Diane whispered.

"They're going, Di!" Tim exclaimed. "Look, they're leaving her! As soon as they go, we can pick them up, and take them to John Mooney! He'll be glad to see them!"

The Uhlan sergeant had raised a hand in signal to his troop, and the men fell in, and set off down the road. Mrs. Mooney watched them, almost unbelievingly. Evidently she had expected to be questioned and cross-questioned, perhaps to be dragged with her children, as prisoners, to one of the concentration camps.

"I wonder what's come over those Uhlans," Diane whispered. "I've never known them to let anyone off as easy as that. There must be some trick behind it.

"Perhaps it's not Mrs. Mooney they want." She was soon to learn what was behind the apparently lenient action of the Purple troopers. They had cantered about a hundred yards down the road, when the sergeant suddenly raised his hand. The troop halted, and at a sharp command they wheeled, facing back toward Mrs. Mooney and her two children.

Diane put a trembling hand on Tim's arm. "They—they're coming back, Tim. I—I thought it was too good to be true!"

Mrs. Mooney, in the road, thrust her two children behind her, as if to protect them. Her face was white, strained.

The sergeant of Uhlans uttered a second crisp command, and the troopers unslung their carbines with swift precision, raised the guns to their shoulders. Diane screamed: "They're going to shoot them down! God, no—"

The sergeant's voice came to them clearly across the field: "Fire!"

WITH THE desperate swiftness of a she-panther guarding her young, Mrs. Mooney shoved her two children away from her, sent them both staggering off the road, just as twenty carbines barked in unison.

The sharp, murderous rattle of that salvo of death rolled across the field toward Diane and Tim. Mrs. Mooney staggered under the impact of the steel-jacketed slugs. Her body stiffened, as blood spurted from a dozen wounds. Then she crumpled, fell in a pitiful, lifeless heap upon the road.

But she had saved her two children. Her quick thrust had sent them hurtling into the field, on the side of the road nearest to Tim and Diane. The two little ones were hidden from the sight of the troopers.

They were not to be left to escape so easily. The sergeant shouted a quick order, and a half dozen of the Uhlans spurred their horses toward the spot where Mrs. Mooney's body lay.

"Shoot down those brats!" the sergeant shouted. "And be quick!"

7

Tim and Diane had spent a dangerous moment, after the rattle of the carbines, in quieting their startled horses. Now the eyes of the boy and the young woman met. The boy's were full of anger and hate; Diane's reflected the horror of the sight she had just witnessed. She put a trembling hand on the boy's arm.

"Tim! We can't let those two children die like that—"

"You're right! We can't, Di! Let's go!"

The troopers were close to the edge of the road now, probing in the wheat for the children, with their bayonets. The wheat was rustling only a few feet away from the troopers, where the children were moving through it, running away as fast as their legs could carry them.

One of the Uhlans grunted to the others, and the six of them spurred into the wheat, their bayonet-tipped carbines held like spears, with which they sent thrust after thrust at the fleeing children. It was prime sport for these sadistic servants of the Purple Emperor. Ever since the mighty armies of the Purple Empire had set foot upon American soil, they had amused themselves in this fashion. Thousands of American men, women and children had died at the whim of these ruthless conquerors; and now that the resistance of the Americans had stiffened, the Purple troops were even more terrible in the methods of torture and death which they devised for those unfortunate civilians in the Occupied Territory.

Mrs. Mooney's swift and cruel murder was not exceptional. She had just died, as many, many others had died in the previous twelve months, merely to provide a little sport for the soldiers of the Emperor. And the two innocent little Mooney children were now being hunted for the same reason. In a moment, if nothing intervened, their pitiful little bodies would be spitted upon the bayonets of the Uhlans, and another American father would be brutally deprived of wife, son and daughter in the space of five minutes.

But those Uhlans had not counted upon the presence of anyone else at their monstrous sport. Tim and Diane swung in their saddles, and drew their guns. The six Uhlans, preoccupied with their hunt, did not see them as they charged toward the road. But the sergeant and the rest of the Purple troopers suddenly glimpsed them, and shouted warning.

The six Uhlans turned, saw the young woman and the boy charging down upon them, and started to raise their carbines with desperate speed. But they were too late. Both Tim and Diane, tight-lipped, bleak-eyed, fired from the hip, emptying their guns into that crowd of six. Twelve slugs smashed into the gross bodies of those troopers, fired with unerring aim. Before the Uhlans could fire a single shot, they were cut down, hurled from their horses. The mounts, frightened by the shooting, and without a guiding hand on their reins, cantered wildly through the wheat, dragging their riders by the stirrups.

THE ATTACK had been so swift and unexpected that the Uhlans had not had a chance to defend themselves. But with the figure of Mrs. Mooney's riddled body still lying in the road, Tim and Diane had felt no urge to give the troopers a chance.

The two children had stopped short at the first shots, and the wheat was still. It was impossible for Tim and Diane to tell just where they were.

"We've got to get them quick!" Tim gasped. "Here come the other Uhlans."

With hoarse shouts of rage, the rest of the troopers, led by their sergeant, were racing toward the spot. The riderless horses of the six dead Uhlans tangled with the troop in the road for a moment, giving the boy and the young woman a bit more time.

Diane spurred through the wheat while calling, "Come out, children! We're friends. We won't harm you!"

Now the sergeant and the troopers were closer, spurring madly, firing their carbines as they came. Bullets whined close to Diane and Tim as they searched frantically through the wheat for the Mooney children. In a moment they would have to flee for their own lives.

Diane pushed her mount ahead, and cried out triumphantly, as she almost ran down the two little things. They were crouching on the wet ground, huddled in each other's arms, faces streaked with tears. They shrank back from the horses' forefeet, but Diane leaned far down, called to them urgently:

"Come quickly, you little darlings. We'll take you away from those bad men!"

The girl, who was the older of the two, stood up, and put out her arms. Diane smiled, reached down and lifted her up to the saddle, in front of her. Tim spurred around her, and did the same for the little boy. The Uhlans were close now, hardly twenty yards separating them from their quarry.

Tim shouted: "Okay, Di!" and slapped Diane's mount on the rump. The horse leaped ahead through the wheat, and Tim followed, keeping one arm tightly clasped around the waist of the little boy in front of him.

Neither he nor Diane had had a chance to reload their emptied guns; nor did they risk doing so now, with their additional burdens. They spurred their horses on, racing them to the limit, crashing through the trembling wheat on to the hard-packed road, with bullets from the carbines of the Purple Uhlans whining about them. They headed eastward, driving their mounts with every ounce of energy and strength in their bodies.

Both the girl on Diane's pommel and the boy on Tim's horse kept utter silence. They had seen their mother dragged from their home, and they were both numbed with the horror of it, hardly understanding yet all that they had seen.

The pursuing Uhlans were strung out in a long line behind the fugitives, the foremost one being less than fifty feet away. They were riding madly, vindictively, attempting to reload their carbines in the saddle. It was this that saved Tim and Diane and their two little charges from death—the fact that the Purple troopers had already emptied their own guns; otherwise they must surely have been hit at that short distance, even in spite of the fact that they were moving so swiftly.

As it was, they gained a few yards on the troopers, and won a moment's respite by swinging around a curve in the road, which hid them temporarily from sight. Diane called back to Tim, over her shoulder: "Let's take to the fields—"

"Nix!" he shouted. "Straight ahead, Di!"

He pointed forward, toward where the road topped a slight

rise, and skirted a cemetery. There seemed little hope of escaping the pursuit for long, but it was evident that the boy preferred that they remain on the open road rather than be hunted like rabbits in the wheat fields.

Diane sensed his intent, and spurred swiftly ahead. Behind them the Uhlans swung around the bend, grimly silent now, intent on catching up with the fugitives. It was apparent that they must be caught sooner or later. This was all occupied territory. The State of Kansas had long ago become the Province of Kansas, with a viceroy appointed by Emperor Rudolph I. The Purple troops ruled here with an iron hand, and there were few places of refuge for those who defied them.

But Diane and Tim kept on with grim determination. Their horses' hooves clattered on the road as they raced toward the cemetery. But the Uhlans were gaining on them, because their horses were carrying a double load, and they were hampered by the squirming, terror-stricken children.

They came abreast of the cemetery, and the leading Uhlan was less than fifteen feet behind them. It was the sergeant, and he was leaning forward over his pommel, taking careful aim at Tim's back with a long-barreled service revolver.

Tim glanced behind, saw his danger, and swerved his mount, so as to make of himself as difficult a target as possible. The sergeant grinned evilly, and lowered his sight. He chose to shoot Tim's horse. Tim's face was drawn, taut. If his horse went down, the calamity would be as great as if he himself were hit. The boy he was carrying would be hurled to the ground and possibly killed. If the child were not killed by the fall, the fate which the

12

Purple Troopers would mete out to the little shaver would be no better.

Diane, racing ahead, close to the cemetery wall, glanced behind, saw the situation, and slowed up. Tim shouted to her: "Keep going, Di! One of us had to get away. Remember the appointment with Mooney—"

The wind tore the words out of his mouth, and he didn't know if Diane had heard him. But the roar of the sergeant's revolver cut through his shout, and he felt his horse stagger, its stride broken. It had been hit!

He clasped the little boy about the waist, prepared to leap if the horse showed signs of going down. But it limped on, at a staggering, slow pace. The sergeant came abreast of him, grinning, and waved his revolver, motioning for him to dismount.

The other troopers streamed past them, keeping after Diane. Tim had a momentary glimpse of her white face, staring backward, full of misery and helplessness.

THESE TWO had been together in many an adventure. The boy, Tim Donovan; and the young woman, Diane Elliot, were closer than brother and sister. They were bound together by many ties, the strongest of which was loyalty to a common leader.

That leader was Jimmy Christopher, known to the rank and file of the defenders of American freedom as Operator 5. It was Operator 5 whose brilliant strategy and resource, courage and stamina, had kept alive the spirit of America during the dark days of the Purple Invasion, when Emperor Rudolph bade fair to become the absolute ruler of our country. It was he who had mobilized an army of defense, and was even now directing a mighty battle at the Continental Divide.

Diane Elliot and Tim Donovan were here on a mission assigned to them by Operator 5. It was their duty to contact various leaders of volunteers in the Occupied Territory, east of the Continental Divide, and give them instructions for a prearranged, simultaneous attack upon the enemy's rear lines, while the American Defense Force launched an assault against the crack divisions of Marshal Kremer.

It was to be America's supreme attempt to break the might of the Purple Empire in the United States; and upon the successful completion of their mission depended the fate of a hundred and fifty thousand American soldiers comprising the American Defense Force—for without the cooperation of these volunteers from the rear, Operator 5 could not hope to crumble the veteran fighting divisions of the Purple Emperor, Rudolph I.

All of this was in the mind of Diane Elliot as she turned her anguished eyes to see Tim Donovan slowing up behind her. He was as good as captured, and he would without doubt be killed, along with the little Mooney boy on his pommel. Every instinct urged her to stop, not to desert Tim at this moment. Yet she also knew that one of them must get through to Mooney and the other leaders whom they were to instruct. *She must go on!*

Her own chances of escaping were slim enough. The Uhlans were close behind her now, and they were firing. Her horse was spent, laboring under the extra burden of the little girl. Frantically she spurred her mount, her lips forming a message—a message to Tim, which he did not hear.

14

"You understand, don't you, Tim?"

She glimpsed Tim Donovan slowly dismounting at the command of the sergeant, saw him helping the Mooney boy down, while the sergeant covered him with his gun.

And then she heard the drumming of the hooves of the troopers' horses as they closed up the gap between them-selves and her. Hopelessly, she realized that she too had lost her chance of escape.

The cemetery wall stretched far ahead at the right of the road, and there was no cover, no place where she could even make a stand. The leading Uhlan almost within reach of her now, shouting to her to halt. The child on her pommel was whimpering now, calling: *"Mama! Mama! I want my mama!"*

Diane's eyes flickered with quick sympathy for the child. "What's your name, dear?" she asked swiftly.

"Marie—"

"Listen carefully, Marie. I'm going to jump off this horse. I want you to hang on. Can you ride a horse?"

"Yes. Daddy taught me and Johnny—"

"Good. Here I go. Remember, ride, and ride fast—do you hear? Ride until you come to some American home. And God go with you!"

She meant to jump from the horse, to lighten the burden. She would give herself up, perhaps in that way give little Marie Mooney a chance at life.

"And if you see your father, tell him—"

But her plan was not destined to succeed. A hoarse, brutal voice almost at her elbow commanded: "Halt! Halt or I shoot!"

One of the troopers was almost abreast of her. The man could easily have shot her, but he was saving the bullet—saving it the way they had done with Anna Mooney.

Diane sighed. So this was to be the end. By their impetuous action in attempting to rescue these two children, they had accomplished nothing except to get themselves captured, killed. Their mission would remain unfulfilled; the American Defense Force would receive no help from the American volunteers behind the enemy lines. Bitterly, Diane reined in her horse.

And it was at that instant that she heard the shrill, high-pitched whine of a rifle bullet.

CHAPTER 2
KANSAS RIFLES SPEAK

THE SHOT had been fired from somewhere in the cemetery—that much she could tell. A scream echoed the shot, and Diane Elliot saw that the sergeant, Tim Donovan's captor, had been hit.

The man screamed once more as he was literally hurled from his horse by the force of the bullet. A second and a third shot sounded, and two more of the Uhlans fell. The man who was covering Diane snarled, and swung toward this new menace. And from behind her, Diane heard Tim Donovan shout: "Ride, Di! *Get going!*"

She turned for a fleeting instant, and saw that Tim had seized the reins of the sergeant's horse, had vaulted into the saddle, and was helping little Johnny Mooney up in front of him.

More and more shots came from the cemetery, and now the Uhlans were answering the fire of the hidden riflemen.

Diane clasped Marie Mooney close to her, and spurred her horse frantically, racing away from the Uhlans, with Tim Donovan close after her. The troopers paid no attention to them. They were busy with the sharpshooters in the cemetery grounds. Now that Diane and Tim were out of the line of fire, more rifles had opened up from the graveyard, and the Uhlans were being hit again and again. Those who had succeeded in reloading their carbines were shooting frantically in reply, but their fire was ineffectual against the storm of whining bullets that smashed into them.

Only seven or eight of the fourteen were left on their horses, and these turned tail, fled back along the road. But they were not to escape. The hail of lead followed them along the road, cutting them down relentlessly.

Abruptly the rifle fire ceased. The last Uhlan was down. Not one of the original twenty who had shot down Mrs. Mooney remained alive!

Tim Donovan and Diane Elliot had pulled up at the side of the road, close to the cemetery wall. They watched the battle wide-eyed, hardly daring to believe that it was true. They had been on the brink of failure and death, and suddenly, miraculously, all that was changed.

Now they saw a half dozen wiry figures arise from behind

various tombstones in the cemetery. Khaki-clad men, lean and grim-visaged, they came across the cemetery, threading their way between tombstones, rifles held in the crook of their arms.

Tim waved to them wildly, and he quickly dismounted, helping little Johnny Mooney to get down. Diane did the same for Marie. In a moment they were enthusiastically shaking hands with their rescuers.

"Gosh," Tim Donovan grinned, "you boys certainly did a good job! We would have been goners!"

One of the six had not stopped to talk to them. He was a tall, weather-beaten man of forty, with a straggling moustache. Upon seeing the two children he uttered a hoarse cry and ran to them, clasped them both in his arms.

"Johnny! Marie!" he said huskily.

As Diane watched him, she felt her eyes suddenly wet with tears. She had no need to be told that this was John Mooney. And there was news of his wife to be given him—news that she could not summon the courage to impart.

The other five men were gleefully surrounding them, asking questions of them, and at the same time congratulating each other on the ambush of the Uhlans.

"We're part of the Fifth Kansas Volunteer Riflemen," one of the men told Diane and Tim. "We were supposed to meet you just north of Page City, but John Mooney got to worrying that maybe you'd meet a Purple patrol, so we rode out a way. And we saw you two riding, hell-bent-for-leather, with those Uhlans after you. So we just snugged in behind the tombstones, and staged the ambush. I guess it's a good thing we rode out, or you'd never have got to Page City."

"You're darned right!" Tim Donovan informed him. "One minute more and it would have been all over!"

JOHN MOONEY left his two children, came over and introduced himself to them. "I've heard of both of you," he said. "You have orders for us from Operator 5?"

Diane nodded, but said nothing. There was a catch in her throat. She saw the unspoken question in Mooney's eyes. Deliberately he had refrained from asking about his wife. Perhaps he guessed—perhaps he dared not ask.

Diane avoided his glance, stepped past him toward the two children. "You poor little dears!" she murmured. Johnny looked a lot like his father, she thought, and Marie must resemble her dead mother. What cruelty, that these two should be deprived of the loving care of a mother—because a savage dictator wished to make himself master of the world!

The tears were streaming down her cheeks now, unrestrained; and Marie put a pudgy hand on her face.

"Your face is wet," she said. "Why are you crying, lady?"

Neither of them had seen their mother shot. They only knew that she had pushed them off the road, and right after that the horrid Uhlans had come poking after them with their pointed bayonets. It would be a dreadful task to make these two little things realize that they were never going to see their mother again—a task fully as hard as the one that Tim Donovan was facing now.

For Tim was trying to break the news to John Mooney.

"Mr. Mooney," the boy was saying, "the orders from Operator 5 can wait. I—I've got to tell you something—"

The American riflemen crowded around him, and suddenly John Mooney's face went white. "It—it's about Anna—my wife?" he asked huskily.

Tim nodded. "Yes."

"She's—"

"She was shot, Mr. Mooney. We saw her shot. These Uhlans did it. We barely managed to get Johnny and Marie away."

John Mooney's hands clenched at his sides. He bit his lower lip until a speck of blood appeared. "Anna!" he groaned.

One of the men put a hand on his shoulder. "It's tough, John."

The words were uttered gruffly, but they hid a world of feeling. These men were all farmers, neighbors, men who grew the wheat that Kansas had been shipping to feed the rest of the nation before the Purple Invasion. They were used to toiling with their hands, and they were not proficient at flowery speeches. Those three words spoke volumes.

John Mooney bowed his head, and turned away. The others left him alone, respecting his grief. Tim Donovan fidgeted from one foot to the other. Though only a boy, he was used to death. He had seen much of it in the past year, had often been close to it himself in company with Jimmy Christopher. And he had seen hundreds of wives and mothers who had lost husbands and sons in the war. But the sight of John Mooney's silent grief tore at his heart.

One of the riflemen whispered to Tim: "The Uhlans are rounding up all the families of the men who have volunteered for the Defense Force. They're either killing them out of hand, or else sending them to concentration camps, which is a little worse than being killed, if you ask me. Anna Mooney was hiding out with the kids until tonight. She was going to make her way to Homer Martinson's farm, where a lot of the men's families are hiding out. But the Uhlans got her first!"

ABRUPTLY, JOHN MOONEY turned back to them. His features were composed, as if he had mastered his grief. But there was a smoldering fire in his eyes.

"Well," he said hoarsely, "I—guess we got to carry on just the same. What are our orders? I've got three hundred men, all armed with rifles, and all dead shots. I've sent out the call for them to meet at the cemetery tonight. What's the plan?"

"You're to march west tonight," Tim Donovan told him. "Today is Monday. You'll have to be careful not to be spotted by enemy patrols, so you'll move slowly. By Wednesday you're to be at Canyon City. If Miss Elliot and I are able to contact everybody on our list, there should be some three thousand men in the vicinity of Canyon City by Wednesday night. Other contingents will meet at Sedalia, at Boulder, and at Laramie. The others will attack the rear of the enemy's lines at zero hour, which will be six-thirty Wednesday evening. At the same time, columns of the American Defense Force will move in from the west, to attack simultaneously with you through a pass in the Continental Divide."

"What do we do?" John Mooney asked.

"Your job will be to see that the enemy reserve divisions are prevented from reinforcing the Purple lines at the spots where

21

DIANE

our columns attack. Here—" Tim Donovan took a sheet of paper and a pencil from his pocket, and drew a rough sketch— "this is the situation now. The enemy reserve divisions are here, between Pueblo and Trinidad. When the attack is launched, Marshal Kremer will probably order them to move to the passes in the Divide where our columns will attack. If these divisions reach the front lines, we'll never be able to break through. That's why you must stop them."

"We'll stop them!" John Mooney said grimly. He listened while Tim gave him detailed instructions.

"You've got to memorize this," Tim told him. "Operator 5's orders are that nothing must be written down. In the event that any one is captured, the enemy must learn nothing of the projected attack."

Mooney repeated the details after him, committing them to memory. "Six-thirty Wednesday evening is zero hour," he finished. "And may God help America!"

"Amen to that!" Tim said fervently. "And now, we've got to go on. We have to find five more men before morning."

"Which way are you heading?" Mooney asked.

"North. Our next stop is at Goodland, where we meet Frank Randolph."

"That's okay," Mooney said. "We've scouted the Goodland road. There are no enemy patrols there. You'll have clear riding. Now, will you do something for me?"

"Sure," Tim said.

"Take my two kids along. The Homer Martinson farm is on the Goodland road. A lot of the men's families are there, and Johnny and Marie will be well taken care of. It's only a side road, and the Purple troops haven't bothered with it, because Goodland was razed to the ground a few months ago, and they don't think there's any life there. That's why we picked the Martinson farm for all our womenfolk." A couple of the men went into the cemetery grounds and returned in a few moments with

six horses, which they had tethered at
the other end of the grounds. Then they
mounted, and rounded up two of the
horses of the dead Uhlans, which Tim
and Diane mounted, each taking one of
the children.

John Mooney shook hands with them.
"I'll be there with the boys at zero hour,
all right!" he said. "Right now, I—I guess we'll ride down the
road a ways, and—and—dig a grave for—Anna." Tim and
Diane said nothing as the six riflemen rode away. There was
nothing that they could say to console this man in the sudden
bereavement which had stricken him. His case was no different
from that of thousands of other men throughout the country,
who had lost wives, children, entire families through the cruel
depredations of the ruthless Purple troops. There was little doubt
that these men would fight to the last ditch when the time came.

And while Tim and Diane rode north toward the Martinson
farm and Good-land, other messengers were riding, far to the
north and far to the south, to spread the word in Wyoming, in
Nebraska, in Montana and in New Mexico, that would bring
thousands upon thousands of farmers, cowhands, miners and
clerks to rally at their appointed stations for zero hour.

The moment of America's great thrust for freedom was at
hand!

CHAPTER 3
GUNS OF THE DEAD

OUTSIDE A tent in American Field Headquarters, Jimmy Christopher, otherwise known as Operator 5, stood in close consultation with General Hank Sheridan.

Wiry, leathery, sun-tanned product of the West, the commanding general of the American Defense Forces was chewing viciously on a briar pipe, while he squinted through a field glass.

"The Purple troops are dug in all along the Continental Divide," he growled, "as far north as the Medicine Bow Range. I tell you, Operator 5, we haven't got enough men to storm their positions."

He pointed dramatically toward a majestically tall, snow-capped mountain, less than five miles away. "We took Byers Peak over there all right, but it cost us eighteen hundred men. It'd cost us ten thousand men to push through Berthoud Pass!"

Jimmy Christopher nodded soberly. "You're right, Hank. But we've exhausted the available supplies of ammunition for our artillery. The enemy positions have to be taken by man-power, and by manpower alone!"

Hank Sheridan frowned. "I don't understand you, Jimmy. Do you want me to sacrifice ten thousand men in order to take Berthoud Pass?"

Operator 5's lean face reflected the weariness of his body. He had not slept the previous night. But his eyes were bright, keen, as they met those of General Sheridan.

"It may not be necessary to lose ten thousand men, Hank," he said softly, "if a little plan of mine works out!"

He drew a pencil and paper from his pocket, sketched rapidly. "This is the situation now.* We have a hundred and fifty thousand men under arms, opposed to perhaps half a million veteran

---

* AUTHOR'S NOTE: Those readers who are familiar with the history of the Purple Invasion of America will recall that the Central Empire, commonly termed by historians, the "Purple Empire," was already the mistress of two-thirds of the world. Beginning as the small, militaristic Central European state of Balkaria, her dictator had made himself emperor, and had then proceeded to conquer Europe and Asia. Then his veteran cohorts had crossed the Atlantic, and we, who had failed to keep pace with the mad armament race of foreign powers, had no means of defense against the super-tanks, the high-speed planes and the mechanized fighting units of the Central Empire. The conquest of America was swift and ruthless. Against the might of the Purple Empire there was pitted the courage and the resource of only one man—Operator 5. The President of the United States had committed suicide when forced to surrender. Our armies were dispersed and beaten, our civilians forced into labor camps, our cities razed to the ground. But Jimmy Christopher, known in the records of the Secret Service as Operator 5, had managed by his courage and daring to fan to life the spirit of defiance that lurked in the heart of every American He had labored mightily to recruit an army of patriotic men, and he had captured San Francisco from the enemy. Then he had pushed on, forcing the Purple troops to retire to the Continental Divide, where they were now dug in. The story of events leading up to the capture of San Francisco was related in the novel entitled, "Revolt of the Lost Legions."

troops of the Purple Empire. The Purple troops have no more ammunition for their big guns than we have, because our civilians in the Occupied Territory have been pretty successful at sabotage. But they are in possession of the strong positions, and it's up to us to dislodge them. Once we push them back from the Continental Divide, we'll have a chance against them."

Hank Sheridan spoke gloomily. "But how are you going to do it? Marshal Kremer has ten divisions of infantry in reserve at Pueblo. He's already issued orders to move them north to bolster up the troops that are holding Berthoud Pass, and Freedom Pass, up here."

"That's true, Hank. But if my plan works, Marshal Kremer won't move those divisions!"

Hank Sheridan eyed him shrewdly. "You've been away for two days. What you been up to, Jimmy?"

Operator 5 smiled. "Look at this sketch. Here's Berthoud Pass, due west of Denver. Way down here, a hundred miles south, is Concha Pass, west of Pueblo. At Pueblo, Kremer has ten divisions of infantry. Now there are only four passes by which we can attack—the others have been destroyed by dynamite. The first three are within a twenty-mile radius of this spot, while Concha is a hundred miles away."

"Okay," said Hank Sheridan. "Kremer has started to move half his reserve divisions up here already. According to our information, they'll be on the march by tomorrow morning—"

Jimmy Christopher was shaking his head. "I don't think they'll start tomorrow, Hank."

"But why not?"

27

"Because I am going to see to it that Kremer learns that we are planning to mass an attack down at Concha Pass. He'll keep his reserves there."

"You mean you're going to give him misinformation?"

"Right. I'm going to arrange it for him to capture a courier with dispatches for our undercover agents in the east. Those dispatches will state that we are staking everything on a thrust at Concha Pass. But in reality, we'll smash at Berthoud!"

Hank Sheridan was still unconvinced. "But even at that, it'll cost us ten thousand men to drive the enemy out of Berthoud—"

"No! That isn't the whole of my plan. You know I've been keeping contact with undercover agents in the Occupied Territory. They've been afraid to rise against the Purple military machine until now, but I've convinced them that the time has come. There are two hundred thousand men in Kansas, Colorado and Wyoming, waiting for the signal to attack the rear of the Purple position. They're only waiting for the word. And that word is going to reach them tomorrow. I've sent messengers to notify them to attack. Zero hour will be Wednesday, at six-thirty!" Sheridan hesitated. "But Marshal Kremer's reserves—"

"Will be cut off from the front lines. I'm throwing a hundred thousand of those civilians in between Kremer's reserves and their front lines. They should be able to hold them until we break through. In the meantime, the other hundred thousand civilians will attack Berthoud Pass from the rear. We'll have the enemy in a vise!" Hank Sheridan's eyes glowed. "You're a great general, Jimmy! If it only doesn't slip up!"

Operator 5's face was hard as granite. "It can't slip up, Hank.

It mustn't slip up! If it does, we might as well resign ourselves to becoming serfs of that madman, Emperor Rudolph!"

HE TURNED slowly and looked east-ward toward the great, impregnable ridges of the Continental Divide. On the plain below them, the tents of the American army were spread as far as the eye could reach. They were waiting for the word that would send them against the firmly entrenched troops of the Purple Empire, in a battle upon which the fate of America would hang.

And that battle, when it took place, would be different from any modern battle since the World War. There would be no booming of big guns, there would be no crashing tanks, no diving pursuit planes or bombers.

For the resources of America had been exhausted or destroyed by the invader. And our own civilians with aching hearts had helped to destroy those oil wells, those munitions plants which the Purple Empire had spared to employ for its own uses. In all of the United States there was not an oil well that could be tapped or a plant capable of manufacturing high-explosive shells.*

---

* AUTHOR'S NOTE: The modern historian of today, delving into the records of this period, is shocked to realize to just what extent our resources were depleted. After the World War of 1914, the United States emerged as the provider for the world. Kansas wheat was shipped to every portion of the globe to feed starving peoples. Nations everywhere sought eagerly to place orders with us for armaments and munitions. We sold wheat, steel, scrap-iron, planes, munitions, to almost every country in Europe and Asia. The Second World War, which occurred as an indirect result of the Spanish

At Emperor Rudolph's orders, operations were being frantically pushed to drill new wells, to build new factories, to erect new steel mills. Given three months more time, the Purple Empire could have new sinews of war. From Europe it was

Civil War, only served to strengthen our position, because we were wise enough to remain neutral. While the nations of the Eastern Hemisphere throttled each other with war-bloodied hands, we expanded our industries, and took advantage of our almost limitless natural resources. Our mistake was in relying upon the vastness of the Atlantic and Pacific to protect us from invasion. Our navy was large, it was true. But who could have foreseen that the war-mad country of Balkaria would conquer Europe and China and Japan, uniting under one flag the fighting sea-strength of England, France, Italy, Russia and Japan? Our navy could not withstand such might. Nor could our armed forces fight against the powerfully mechanized divisions of the Purple Empire. During the first wave of the Purple Invasion, whole cities were destroyed, great manufacturing centers disappeared, and thousands of square miles of agricultural land were reduced to arid waste. Once the Purple troops established their control over the Occupied Territory, they built new factories, and began to operate our oil wells and mines. As a measure of self-protection—to prevent the enemy from using our own resources to destroy us, we were compelled to send our agents into the Occupied Territory to blow up shipyards, to destroy mines and wells, and to cripple industry. It is an established fact that at the time when the two armies faced each other at the Continental Divide, there was not enough gasoline in the whole length and breadth of the country to drive a hundred automobiles for a thousand miles!

rushing fresh supplies of munitions. If the Americans did not crash through quickly, they would never have another chance.

"God help us!" General Hank Sheridan whispered. Suddenly his eyes narrowed. "Look here, Jimmy—you said you're going to arrange for a courier to be captured with fake dispatches. Who's—going to be that courier?"

Operator 5 sighed. "I was afraid you'd get around to asking that, Hank. I couldn't ask anybody to volunteer for certain capture—"

"So you want to go yourself, I suppose?"

"That's it, Hank."

Sheridan's mouth tightened in a stubborn line. "Well, Operator 5, you can just forget about it! I'm not letting you deliberately stick your head in the lion's mouth. Nix! Maybe you don't know that Rudolph has placed a fabulous reward on your head? Maybe you don't know that you'd probably be drawn and quartered if you were captured?"

Jimmy Christopher smiled. "Nevertheless, I'm going. They won't know I'm Operator 5, unless I tell them. And you can depend on me to keep it a secret."

"But Rudolph knows you by sight, and so does Marshal Kremer, and that Prime Minister, Baron Flexner."

"I'll change my appearance a little, Hank. They won't recognize—?"

He paused as the frantic drumming of a horse's hooves sounded behind them.

Hank Sheridan pointed excitedly. "That's Sergeant MacTavish, from the heliograph station! He must have important news!"

The rider raced through the rows of headquarters tents, and fairly flung himself from his mount when he reached them. Sergeant Aloysius MacTavish had been a member of the Royal Canadian Mounted Police, but had volunteered to serve with Operator 5 at the inception of the Purple Invasion. He was tall, lanky, hard-bitten, yet withal he was possessed of a dry sense of humor which endeared him to Operator 5. That sense of humor was not in evidence now as he gasped out his sensational and disastrous news.

McTAVISH

"Jimmy!" he exclaimed. "We've just had a heliograph* flash,

---

* AUTHOR'S NOTE: Telephone and telegraph, electric lighting and water supply had been destroyed. Communication was maintained by means of primitive heliograph, and by courier. Horses were worth their weight in gold, and cavalry had once more become an important fighting unit. Radio was a thing of the past for the time being, since it was impossible to generate enough power to operate a broadcasting station. For a while a few sending sets had been operated by means of storage batteries, but they had given out. We, as well as the Purple Empire, had managed to set up factories to make ammunition for small arms and rifles, and these were the only weapons with which two great armies fought, except for some antiquated cannon on both sides, for which stores of unused ammunition existed. We, as well as the enemy, subsisted upon whatever could be snatched from nature. Thus did a year of destructive warfare wipe out the fruits of centuries of progress!

relayed from our troops in the Medicine Bow Range. The enemy made a surprise march in the night, around the Rocky Mountain National Park, and they've taken us in the flank. They've captured Willow Creek Pass up there, and there's nothing to stop them from pouring their army through the pass and driving straight south!"

Jimmy Christopher gripped his arm. "Are they coming through, yet Mac?"

"Not yet, Jimmy. They're digging in, and waiting for reinforcements—"

Hank Sheridan groaned aloud. "They've got us clean, Jimmy. And it's all my fault. I never expected they'd come around through the Medicine Bow Range, so I moved all the available men over to the Divide. It'll take six or seven hours to move a decent-sized force back to Willow Creek Pass—and by that time they could send a hundred thousand Purple troops through!"

Jimmy Christopher's eyes had been almost shut as he concentrated upon the problem. Now he swung on Sheridan. "Look here, Hank," he exclaimed. "What happened to those old cannon that used to be on the parade grounds in the Presidio in San Francisco? Didn't you haul them out here?"

Sheridan nodded miserably. "Yes. And we brought a load of cannon balls along. They're relics of the Spanish American War. The chances are, they'd explode if they were fired—"

"We'll have to chance that. If I'm not mistaken, you were hauling them across to the Rocky Mountain National Park. Are they there now?"

"They're on the way. They should be somewhere around Willow Creek Pass now—"

"Right! Now listen—Park View Peak is only a couple of miles from Willow Creek Pass. It commands the pass, doesn't it?"

"Sure. But—"

"Never mind the 'buts!'" He swung to MacTavish. "Heliograph up there, Mac. Catch those old cannon, and have them moved up to Park View Peak. I want them mounted on the summit of the Peak, and if the Purple troops try to come through, fire the damned things. It's a long chance, but if they don't explode, they ought to hold the enemy back until we can move some troops in there!"

MacTavish nodded. "Right, Operator 5. Anything else?"

"Yes. Send a heliograph message to Colonel Smithfield's Fifth Oregon Cavalry at Monarch Lake. I want him to mount his whole regiment and ride like hell to Willow Creek Pass. I'm going to use one of the scout planes and fly up there. I want Colonel Smithfield to meet me at Park View Peak in three hours, with every available man he can mount. Get going, Mac!"

MacTavish leaped on his horse, and clattered away.

Hank Sheridan asked: "What do you figure on doing, Jimmy?"

"If those old cannon can hold the enemy from coming through for the next three hours," Operator 5 told him, "I'm going to dislodge them from the pass."

"And I suppose you'll want to lead the attack?"*

---

* AUTHOR'S NOTE: Readers familiar with the incidents of the early days of the Purple Invasion will remember than Hank Sheridan who was then the

Jimmy Christopher smiled at him. "I wouldn't send Smith-field's men in any place that I wouldn't go myself, Hank."

Sheridan returned his smile coldly. "Well, you won't, Operator 5? We need you here."

"Sorry, Hank, but this is my show—"

"And I say you can't go!"

"Try to stop me!" Operator 5 barked and strode off toward the waiting plane, without looking back.

CHAPTER 4
THE BATTLE OF
MEDICINE BOW

OPERATOR 5'S pilot set him down in a clearing just below Park View Peak, within sight of Willow Creek Pass. He instructed the pilot to go up over the pass and report as to the number of enemy troops concentrated on the other side of the Medicine Bow Range.

After the plane took off, Jimmy Christopher turned to the

mayor of a small western town, had organized a desperate resistance against the invader, and made his name immortal at the battle of Snyder Pass. After that he rose rapidly in the ranks of the American Defense Force, until he was given full command of the field forces. His relationship with Operator 5 was peculiar. Realizing that Jimmy Christopher was far superior to him as a military strategist, he had repeatedly tried to turn the command over to him. But Operator 5 felt that he could accomplish far more as a free-lance, and had consistently refused the position.

young lieutenant who had been waiting there for him. The young chap saluted snappily. "Lieutenant Wilson, sir," he said, "of Captain Storm's Northern Wyoming Riflemen. We were moving those old cannon, and we got your orders to install them on the Peak, here. We've got two of them to the top now, with mules. There are six more waiting to go up."

"How much ammunition have you got?" Jimmy demanded.

"About twenty rounds for each gun, sir. Captain Storm is wondering if they'll shoot. We haven't had occasion to use them yet."

"We'll soon find out," Jimmy Christopher told him. "Keep two of the cannon down here. Build earthworks around them, in case the enemy should break through. Have they shown signs of coming through the pass yet?"

"No, sir. They must be waiting for reinforcements. They're digging in."

Operator 5 glanced toward the pass. About a hundred of the Northern Wyoming Riflemen had advanced over the rocky terrain, and he could spot their figures, where they had taken shelter behind rocks and crags, within rifle range of the exit from the pass.

As Jimmy watched, he saw a small patrol of Central Empire troopers appear on the road, coming out from the pass. Puffs of smoke suddenly spurted from dozens of rifles. At this distance from the pass the sound did not reach, but Jimmy could see the effects; for several figures among the patrol were hit, and collapsed on the road. The rest of them retreated precipitately.

"Good boys!" Operator 5 said. "How many men have you got altogether, Lieutenant?"

"Two hundred and fifty, sir. Captain Storm is at the top of the Peak, with the cannon. And there's the third one, going up now, provided the old wheels last."

He pointed toward the foot of the peak, where a long string of mules were dragging an antiquated piece of ordnance up the winding road. "It takes about two hours to get one of them to the top. I—"

He broke off as the droning of a plane's motor sounded above them. Jimmy's pilot was returning, flying low over the pass. Jimmy watched him come around into the wind and land, and then ran over to the plane. The pilot climbed out.

"It looks bad, Operator 5," he reported. "There's about fifteen hundred men digging in at the pass here. I flew about twenty miles north, and spotted a heavy force of enemy troops coming down around the northern end of Chambers Lake. Must be a whole division, mostly infantry."

Jimmy frowned. "If Smithfield's regiment doesn't get here quick, we'll have a tough job taking the pass. Once they get that division dug in, the odds'll be all against us."

Lieutenant Wilson had left him to superintend the throwing up of the breastworks for the two cannon, under the shadow of the mountain. There was a short gully at the edge of the flying field, and it was this spot that he had chosen.

Operator 5 glanced at his watch impatiently. Smithfield's Fifth Oregon Cavalry should be here shortly. Other regiments would be coming in during the day, as Hank Sheridan succeeded in contacting them. And in the meantime, everything depended on whether these old cannon would shoot with sufficient effect. Jimmy was taut, nervous. The enemy had fifteen hundred men in that pass now, and they were opposed by a paltry two hundred and fifty riflemen. They were making a mistake in waiting for reinforcements to come up before advancing. Of course, the delay was tactically correct, but Jimmy hoped that their commander would not decide to push his advantage and surprise the Americans.

HE CROSSED over to where Wilson was working in the gully. The lieutenant had forty or fifty of his young Wyoming riflemen sweating with pick and shovel to throw up a protective trench, while twenty or thirty others were packing two earthen emplacements for the guns.

The cannon had been carried in six mule-drawn wagons. They brought one of the wagons down into the gully, and everybody lent a hand to the task of mounting the first of the guns. It was a good half hour before the field piece was in place. Jimmy ordered the wagon parked in such a position that it would screen the activity from any enemy observers on the ridges of the Medicine Bow Mountains. If they got wind of the fact that the Americans were preparing cannon, it might serve to precipitate their attack.

At last the gun was mounted to Operator 5's satisfaction. Captain Storm came down from the top of Park View Peak, and shook hands with Jimmy.

"We've got a precious small store of powder, Operator 5," he said. "But there ought to be enough to fire for twenty rounds. These old muzzle-loaders may go off the wrong way, but it's worth a chance. I've had them sandpapered inside and outside, and the fire-vents cleaned with kerosene. Outside of that, there's nothing I could do with them."

"That'll have to be enough," Jimmy grinned.

"Shall we try shooting this one?" Lieutenant Wilson asked.

"Certainly not!" Operator 5 told him. "What the enemy doesn't know won't hurt them. Wait till they start coming through, then we'll start shooting."

"It may be as much of a surprise for us as for them!" Captain Storm grunted. "I've got two of the cannon all set, about halfway up the Peak, here, and I've got signalmen every two hundred yards on the road, to relay the signal to fire. The men are using a fuse to set off the first charge, so they won't be blown to Kingdom Come if the damned things fall apart!"

"Good idea!" Jimmy approved. "Let's do the same here."

They set up a length of fuse, loaded the gun, and then set to work laying the second piece.

The men were all serious, quiet. They realized the gravity of the situation. They came from all parts of Wyoming, and many of them had left wives and children in enemy territory east of the Divide, to come and serve with the American Defense Force. They understood that the enemy must have pushed through Eastern and Northern Wyoming in order to reach this section of the Medicine Bow Range—and that meant only one thing— that the Purple troops had pillaged, looted, murdered, as they did wherever they marched. Many of these men knew in their hearts that they would never see their families alive again; and a great bitterness showed in the tight set of the mouths, in the grim, bleak look of their eyes. Hardy veterans of the timberlands and the cattle country, they were all expert riflemen, and would give a good account of themselves in a battle. But Operator 5 wondered how long these two hundred and fifty men could last against the fifteen hundred Purple troops in the pass. Everything depended on the guns, until Colonel Smithfield's regiment should show up.

Captain Storm must have been thinking of the same thing, for he said: "I hope to God the cavalry gets here soon. My boys are very bitter, and if the enemy should attack, there'd be no holding them back. They'd fight like madmen, and probably get massacred—"

He was interrupted by the shrill blast of a whistle. A lookout on the road leading up to the top of the peak had sounded the warning. Now the lookout was gesticulating toward the pass.

Jimmy Christopher and Captain Storm glanced in the direction in which the man was waving, and Jimmy's eyes narrowed. The enemy was advancing!

Captain Storm exclaimed excitedly: "Here they come!"

THE PURPLE troops, in two columns, were marching out of the pass. They were coming at the double-quick, and a high-shakoed major of Purple Infantry rode at their head upon a black horse. Two drummers followed him, beating the quick marching time of the Purple Army. Those drums had crossed America, and were a familiar and hateful sight to every American; for upon their sides was painted in black the fearful insignia of the Central Empire—the severed head and the crossed broadswords. This was the insignia of the Purple flag, under which the

Emperor of the Central Empire had marched to conquest over the dead and mangled bodies of millions of people.

And now that flag and those drums were at the head of a column moving to disperse a brave but pitiably small force of Wyoming volunteers. Once the Wyoming riflemen were scattered, the way would be open for division after division of Marshal Kremer's goose-stepping troops to sweep down upon the flank of the American Defense Force.

Captain Storm's riflemen were firing at the moving column, and Operator 5 could see puffs of smoke from behind a hundred crags and boulders. A few Purple troopers began to fall before the accurate shooting of the riflemen, but the column kept moving. The major was down, and one of the drummers. The riflemen kept up their fire.

But suddenly, a dreadful barrage of carbine fire began to beat down upon the Wyoming riflemen from the high spots in the Medicine Bow Mountains. A veritable hail of lead swept down upon the Wyoming men, driving them back behind their shelter. The enemy had posted sharpshooters and snipers up there, to cover the advance of the column!

Captain Storm exclaimed: "We can't stop them with rifle fire, Operator 5. My boys will be shot to the last man if they expose themselves to take aim." He groaned. "And look—that's just what they're doing! See, they're madmen—they don't care if they're hit, as long as they get one of the enemy—"

Operator 5 interrupted him. "Signal your men at the top to open up with the cannon, Captain! They must aim at the pass, and not at the men who are already through. The object is to keep more of them from coming out!"

Captain Storm nodded, and began to wigwag to the signal-man on the road above.

Jimmy Christopher sprang to the one cannon they had succeeded in setting up, and knelt behind it, laid his sights carefully. The enemy was moving forward swiftly now, spreading out as they left the mouth of the pass. The major was on foot now. It appeared that his horse had been hit, and not he. Three or four hundred had come through already, and the mouth of the pass was choked with Purple troops when Operator 5 finally stood up, and nodded, satisfied. "Set it off!" he ordered. One of Captain Storm's men stooped to light the fuse, which had been laid to a point about ten feet away, in order to give everyone a chance to get out of the way in case the gun should explode. Jimmy Christopher's eyes narrowed. That fuse would take a precious three minutes to burn. In three minutes, three hundred additional Purple troopers would be through the pass.

He waved the man away, sprang to the gun and drew out his clasp knife. He slashed off the fuse close to the breech, lit a match and applied it to the end of the fuse. The riflemen, seeing what he was about to do, had begun to run back. Now Jimmy sprang away, just as the fuse ignited the powder.

There was a quick flash, followed by a sudden detonation. Jimmy Christopher, not three feet from the gun, waited to see if its casing would explode into a thousand fragments.

BUT THE old cannon did not explode. It recoiled with a crash, and smoke poured from its muzzle as the projectile was hurtled outward. A cheer went up from the Wyoming riflemen, as the shot landed square in the mouth of the pass, among the close-pressed troops there. Flesh and bones of the enemy were scattered in a wild flare of flame, and smoke enveloped the spot.

When the smoke cleared, the ground was seen to be strewn with the twisted bodies of Purple troopers, while hundreds of their fellows were fleeing pell-mell back into the pass.

The Wyoming men shouted themselves hoarse, and at that instant, the two cannon up on the peak rumbled their defiant roar of the Purple Empire, sending two more projectiles into the pass. These were a little high, and they struck the sides of the overhanging cliffs, sending a shower of rock and debris down upon the fleeing enemy troopers.

The two or three hundred Purple soldiers who were already out of the pass saw that they were cut off from their fellows, and immediately took cover, wherever they could find it, returning the hot fire of the Wyoming riflemen.

Jimmy Christopher shouted to Captain Storm: "Keep up a barrage on the mouth of the pass! Don't let any more of them through!"

Then he ran down to the end of the gully, vaulted on to one of the horses which were tethered there, and raced across the open ground toward the pass. About a quarter mile to the south he had spotted a body of cavalry, riding madly toward them. That would be Smithfield's Oregon regiment. Now was the time to counter-attack, while the enemy had not yet reformed. Smithfield's regiment would be able to come up in time to support him.

The Wyoming riflemen, seeing him ride toward the pass, rose up from behind their shelter, and fell in behind him, disregarding the pot shots of the enemy, who had taken shelter all around them.

Carbine bullets whined around Operator 5's head, but he did not swerve from his course, heading directly for the pass. The wildly shouting riflemen could not keep up with him, but they came on, irresistibly, firing as they ran, mopping up those of the enemy troops at whom they could get a shot.

Jimmy reached the mouth of the pass, saw ahead of him a trench, and cut squarely into the road ahead of him. The trench had been dug some fifty feet back from the mouth of the pass, and he could see the round-helmeted heads of the Purple troops peering over the top. They were shooting at him now from that trench, but Jimmy rode on grim-lipped, while behind him the swiftly approaching cavalry regiment of Colonel Smithfield had outstripped the Wyoming riflemen.

The Oregon horsemen were close behind him now, but Jimmy was forced to rein in, because of the crater in the road, caused by the projectile he had fired from the old cannon.

Operator 5 flung himself from his horse, slapped it on the rump, sending it off the road. In back of him he heard a stentorian voice shouting a command: "Prepare to dismount! Dismount! Fix bayonets! Prepare to charge. At the double-quick—*charge!*"

He glanced behind him, while a hail of lead from the enemy

trench whined all about him. White-mustached, white-haired Colonel Smithfield was less than twenty feet behind him, charging at the head of his men.

This regiment of Oregon cavalry had been recruited from timber lands and gold mines, from dairy farms and fishing fleets. The men wore every conceivable sort of uniform, but they were all equipped with rifles, and there was not a man among them who did not know how to use a bayonet.

Colonel Smithfield waved to Jimmy Christopher. "Carry on, Operator 5!" he shouted. "We're with you!"

Jimmy grinned, yanked the revolver from his holster, and ran toward the enemy trench, bending low. The steel-helmeted Purple troops fired frantically, swiftly, and inaccurately. They were not used to hand-to-hand fighting. Always their attacks had been preceded by a barrage of artillery fire that had cleaned up the terrain ahead of them. Now, faced with the prospect of fighting these determined, burly men from Oregon, they were panic-stricken, confused. They fired too soon, and did little damage to the attackers. Although they had the advantage of being dug in, they were taken by surprise in that they had expected to be the aggressors instead of the defenders in this engagement.

Jimmy Christopher leaped the last remaining two feet which intervened between himself and the trench. He had emptied his gun, and now he reversed it, smashing at faces with the butt, warding off bayonets with his elbow. All about him now the Oregon men were locked in hand-to-hand struggle with the Purple troopers and no one asked for or gave quarter in the furious swirling mêlée. He hurled his empty revolver into the face of an enemy sergeant, then stooped and picked up the carbine of a dead Purple soldier. Its bayonet was red with the blood of some American, but Operator 5, fighting like a cold, calculating fighting machine, soon joined that blood to the blood of the enemy. All these Americans were charging with the cold hard fury of men who had heard dreadful tales of the cruel inhumanity of these Purple troopers, and who gloried in the chance to pay back for the millions of Americans who had died or suffered torture at the hands of Rudolph's servants.

NO PRISONERS were taken. The trench was cleared in five minutes. And the Americans swarmed over the top, pursuing the escaping enemy, driving them back up the mountains, or farther into the road. Ahead the full force of the enemy could be seen concentrating to meet the onslaught of the Oregonians. They were massed in close order, in the famous square formation which Marshal Kremer had developed, and by means of which he had won battle after battle in three continents.

But the Americans were not to be stopped today. They broke that square as if it had been a thing of papier-mâché. The Wyoming riflemen had joined the fray, and they were cleaning up the hidden snipers and sharpshooters. Within thirty minutes of the firing of that first cannon, Willow Creek Pass was once more in the hands of the Americans.

The grisly ensign of the Purple Empire was hauled down from the hut of the commanding major, and the Stars and Stripes went up, amid hoarse cheers.

The Americans had lost ninety men in the battle, the Purple

Empire four hundred and thirty. The rest were in full retreat, a wild disorderly rout toward Chambers Lake, where they hoped to meet the Purple reinforcing divisions.

Jimmy Christopher did not push the pursuit, although both Colonel Smithfield and Captain Storm urged it.

"We haven't a strong enough force to work far into the enemy territory," he told them. "You'd only be cut off. And that would endanger our big plan for Wednesday night."

Briefly, he explained to him what he had in mind for Wednesday. "Use the trenches the enemy built here, and dig in. Hold them off till six-thirty Wednesday. Then you can join the big push. In the meantime I'm going through the pass into the Occupied Territory."

"You're—*what?*" Colonel Smithfield demanded.

Jimmy smiled. "I'm going to use a little make-up, so I won't be so easily recognized. I've got some fake dispatches in my pocket. I'm going through, and let myself be captured by Kremer's men. Those dispatches, if Kremer swallows them, will influence him, to keep his reserves at Pueblo, instead of moving them up north. On Wednesday, we'll attack at Berthoud Pass before he can bring up his reserves!"

"Damned good idea!" Smithfield approved. "But what of you? They'll kill you!"

Jimmy Christopher shrugged. "I'll have to hope for a break—"

Captain Storm suddenly snapped his fingers. "I've got it!"

"You've got what?"

Storm smiled. "You know I talk the language of the Purple Empire pretty well. I have forty or fifty men who can talk it as well as I can. We'll take the uniforms of these dead troopers, and follow you into the Occupied Territory. After you're captured, we'll do our damned-est to pull a rescue!"

Jimmy hesitated. "It's a wild scheme, and I don't want you to take the risk—

"Risk, hell!" Storm scoffed. He swung toward his men, called out: "How many volunteers can I get from the Northern Wyoming Rifles, to go into the Occupied Territory?"

Every hand went up. Storm turned to Jimmy Christopher, triumphantly.

"You see? You can't deprive the boys of their chance. Say it's a deal!"

Jimmy gulped. These men were willing to risk their lives, merely on the chance that they might be able to help him. He couldn't refuse them. "It's a deal!" he said. A ringing cheer went up from the men as he and Storm shook hands.

"I'm taking you for two reasons," he told the captain. "There's myself, of course; and there are also some very good friends of mine, whom I've already sent on a very dangerous mission. They're to meet John Mooney, and some other civilians behind the enemy lines, and give the word for the attack at zero hour. They're almost sure to be caught before they complete their mission. And perhaps, if I have your help, I will be able to do something for them."

"Whatever happens to us in there," Storm told him grimly, "we won't die easy. Wyoming men are hard to kill!"

CHAPTER 5
A "MESSAGE TO GARCIA"

WHILE OPERATOR 5 was deliberately preparing to invite capture by Marshal Kremer's men, Diane Elliot and Tim Donovan rode slowly northward in Kansas.

Little Johnny Mooney had fallen asleep on Tim Donovan's pommel, and Tim jogged along carefully, so as not to wake the little shaver. Diane Elliot tried to cheer up Marie Mooney, who was riding with her. Marie was old enough to realize that there was dreadful danger. Though she had not seen her mother shot, the child guessed that something had happened to her.

Marie's wide blue eyes were on the verge of filling with tears as she looked up trustfully at Diane. "D-do you think I'll meet my mama at the Martinson Farm?" she asked.

Diane stroked her hair, while she guided the horse with one hand. "Don't you worry, Marie. Everything will be all right. There'll be some nice ladies at the Martinson Farm, and they'll take care of you fine, till your daddy comes back."

Try as she would, she could not bring herself to tell this child that she would never see her mother again. Diane had risked her life a hundred times in the service of the country, and she had stared death in the face with poise and courage. But she shrank from the task of telling a little girl that her mother was dead.

The child rested her head on Diane's shoulder, and they rode

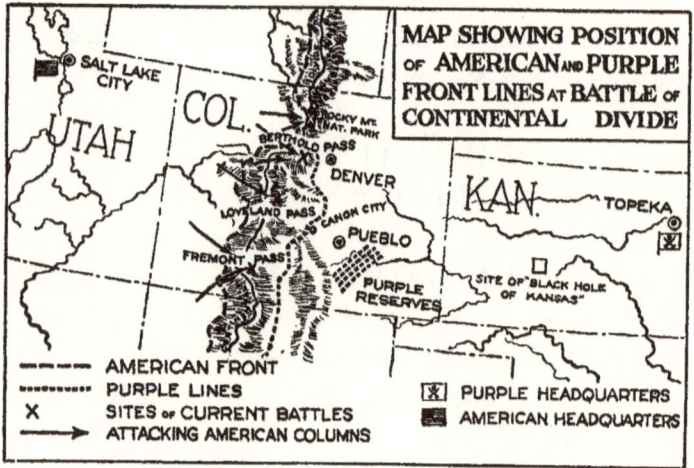

on in silence. Tim Donovan pushed up alongside her, and whispered across: "We'll have to separate at the Martinson Farm, Di, or else we'll never be able to reach all our men."

Diane nodded. "You're right, Tim. We should be there soon. You go north, and I'll go west."

They were passing through a stretch of back country that had suffered heavily in the original invasion. Nothing was visible for miles in every direction but flat, neglected fields, with here and there the charred remains of a farm house or barn. Half a dozen times they passed automobiles deserted at the side of the narrow dirt road.

These cars had been driven as far as they would go with the available supply of gasoline, and had then been left where they stopped.

It was late in the afternoon when Tim and Diane came in sight of the Martinson Farm. It was one of the few buildings that had remained standing in this section of the country. The wheat fields had not been razed, and the wheat grew high on three sides of the farmhouse, which was about a hundred feet back from the road.

They saw the building as they came around a bend in the dirt road, about a half mile away. No smoke came from its chimney, and there were no signs of life. Anyone passing might have thought that it was as deserted as was everything else hereabouts. But as their horses drew closer, a woman stepped out suddenly from behind a tree.

She was a big woman, and she was dressed in a man's worn jacket and trousers. Under her arm she carried an old lever-action Winchester rifle, and there was a hunting knife stuck in her belt. She raised the rifle to bar them, and Diane, who was in the lead, reined in.

The woman started to demand: "Who are you—" but her eyes focused on little Marie Mooney, and she abruptly exclaimed: "Marie! Darling!" and ran to Diane's horse, helped the child off.

Marie said: "Hello, Mrs. Martinson. My brother Johnny is here, too. We've come to stay with you."

Mrs. Martinson took Johnny Mooney down from Tim's horse, and asked: "Where's your mother, Marie?"

Then she looked up, and what she saw in Diane's eyes made her suddenly go pale. Her lips formed the question: *"Dead?"*

Diane nodded, then dismounted and swiftly whispered to her the story of what had happened.

Mrs. Martinson clasped the two children to her ample bosom.

"You poor little darlings! Come on up to the house, and I'll give you something hot to eat. Wait till I get myself relieved."

She put two fingers to her lips, and whistled shrilly, once. "That's the signal that I want a relief sentry," she explained to Diane. "We keep watch day and night. There's no telling when the Purple troops may discover this hideout of ours."

WHILE THEY waited, Diane introduced herself and Tim, related to her the story of how they had got here, and what their mission was.

Mrs. Martinson listened with avid interest. "May God grant you success!" she breathed fervently. "We haven't got much in the way of rations, but you're welcome to anything we have. You must stay a while—"

Diane shook her head. "We must be on our way. A cup of coffee, if you have it—"

A young girl with another antiquated rifle appeared to relieve Mrs. Martinson, and they started for the house.

"We have a hundred and nine women here," Mrs. Martinson explained, "and seventy-seven children. They've come in from neighboring towns and farms. The Uhlans have been going around and arresting or shooting all those women and children whose husbands did not report to work on the forced labor drafts. Those are the men who have gone to join the American Defense Force."

"How about your husband, Mrs. Martinson?" Tim Donovan asked.

She sighed. "He died in the early days of the war—at Snyder

Pass. He fought under General Hank Sheridan. Since then, I've been doing my bit here behind the lines."

They neared the house now, and Diane and Tim saw that the women here had provided for the possibility of being discovered by the Uhlans. Most of the windows were boarded up, with loopholes to shoot through. A covered runway had been built from the rear of the building to an artesian well some hundred feet behind the house. A few of the women were doing chores in the grounds, but next to each of them there rested a rifle, within arm's reach.

"It's like the old days of the pioneers," Mrs. Martinson told Tim and Diane bitterly. "We've got to be on the watch every minute of the day and night, just the way the old settlers had to look out for Indians. Only now, they're Uhlans instead of Indians, and you can take my word for it that they're a hundred times worse. If they don't scalp, they torture."

"I don't have to take your word for it, Mrs. Martinson," Diane told her somberly. "I've seen those Uhlans in action!"

Inside the house, heavy pieces of timber were buttressing the boardings on the windows, and hogsheads of water were stored everywhere in the event that the communication to the well should be broken.

"We have a special store of food for the kiddies, and plenty of hardtack and canned corn and beans, which we don't touch now. That's in case we're attacked. We could stand a siege here for a week or two, at least."

Tim Donovan looked around doubtfully. Mrs. Martinson saw his disapproving glance. "What's eating you, youngster?"

she demanded. "Don't you like the arrangements? You're only a boy, but I hear that Operator 5 places a lot of confidence in you. Speak up!"

Tim Donovan shifted uncomfortably. "I don't like to criticize you, Mrs. Martinson. You're doing a brave job of hiding out all these women and children. But I'm afraid if you were discovered by the Uhlans, you wouldn't last twenty-four hours!"

There were fifteen or twenty women in the huge living room, many of them nursing small babies at their breasts, others knitting, or polishing rifles. They all stared questioningly at Tim. Mrs. Martinson had introduced Tim and Diane to them, and they knew who the lad was.

Tim Donovan looked around the room diffidently. "You see," he explained, "the Uhlans wouldn't really have to attack this house to get at you. All they'd have to do would be to wait for a favorable wind, and set fire to the wheat field. The wheat is growing so close to the house that the building would be sure to catch fire!"

There was a moment of startled silence in the room. Then the women burst into a babble of excited talk. "The boy is right! We should have thought of that before. Good God, they could burn us out like rats!"

THE WOMEN were not to blame for having overlooked such an obvious weakness in their defense. Though they were brave enough, they lacked the necessary experience in warfare. Tim Donovan, on the other, even though he was still in his 'teens, planned and fought with the benefit of a long and hard training under Operator 5. Many years ago, Jimmy Christopher had taken the boy under his wing, attracted to him by the lad's natural intelligence and quickness to learn.

He had taught the boy how to shoot, how to ride, how to transmit and receive Morse and International Code, in addition to a hundred other little tricks; so that Tim Donovan could handle himself with the sureness and swiftness of an experienced Intelligence agent. It was this ability which had brought Tim the present assignment from Operator 5. Americans everywhere knew the boy, knew of his association with Operator 5, and respected him for the confidence which they knew Jimmy Christopher placed in him. That respect was invariably increased when they saw the lad in action.

Now, as Tim's suggestion grew on the women defenders of the Martinson Farm, they set to work at once to rectify the defect. Mrs. Martinson exclaimed: "Come on, girls! Get hold of some scythes from the cellar. We'll cut down the wheat for fifty feet around the house!"

While two dozen of the women volunteered for this work, Mrs. Martinson took Tim and Diane upstairs, showed them the upper part of the house. The second floor, as well as the attic, had been fitted out as a dormitory to accommodate the hundred and nine women and the seventy-seven children. Mattresses had been laid on the floor, and screens had been placed around them at suitable intervals, to provide a bit of privacy.

In one corner of the upper floor, near the window facing west, a screen was set up about a single bed.

"That," Mrs. Martinson explained, "is Mrs. Slocum's bed. Her husband was killed two weeks ago—by a firing squad. And she's going to give birth to a baby in a very short while."

Diane sighed. No matter what events shook the world, disrupting whole nations and whole continents, life went on just the same. Here was an infant about to be brought into the world, while men died in battle, and while women and children hid for their lives. What would be the future of Mrs. Slocum's little baby when it was born? Would it grow up to live and die as a serf of the Purple Emperor, or would it become a free American man or woman, proud of a country that had driven out a vicious invader?

Fiercely, Diane resolved that she would do everything in her power—even to giving her life—to make America once more a free land in which children could grow up in the tradition of American liberty and not of foreign dictatorship and slavery.

On the way downstairs, Tim managed to whisper to her: "I don't like this whole set-up, Di! Even when they cut down the wheat, they won't be safe here. As long as the Uhlans don't discover them, they're all right. But they'll never be able to hold out for a week. The Purple army still has a little ammunition left for their big guns—and one shell would wipe out this whole place!"

Diane glanced at the broad back of Mrs. Martinson, who was preceding them down the stairs. "But what can we do about it, Tim? You and I can't spare any time, anyway. We've got to be going."

"If there was only some way to get these women and children through the lines—"

He stopped abruptly as the piercing shrill of a whistle sounded outside—once, twice, three times!

Mrs. Martinson uttered a gasp. "That's the danger signal!" She raised her voice in a shout that was heard throughout the house: "Everybody to your battle stations! Open the door to let the women in, and be ready to shut it at once!"

THE SOUND of rapid firing came from outside. A woman shrieked somewhere. A bullet smashed into the outer wall of the house.

Tim and Diane ran to a window, peered out. A squadron of mounted Uhlans streaming down the dirt road toward the house, in column of twos. The girl who had relieved Mrs. Martinson as sentry was running from them, trying to reach the house. As they watched, Tim and Diane saw the girl shot down from behind. She stumbled, with a bullet in her back, and fell headlong. In an instant the horses of the troopers trampled her down, crushing her poor dead body. The Uhlans swung off the road toward the house, their carbines spitting fire, belching lead.

The women within the building had already taken their stations at windows and loopholes, on both floors as well as in the attic. They were answering the fire, and two or three of the troopers fell from their mounts.

Mrs. Martinson was at the door, holding it open, while the women from the fields, and those who had been cutting the wheat, streamed in. The last of the women darted in through the open door, and Mrs. Martinson slammed it shut, but not before a hail of lead had poured in from the carbines of the Uhlans.

Two of the women at the opposite end of the room were

wounded by the sudden burst, and another woman, who had been carrying an infant up the stairs to the protection of the upper floors, was also hit. The woman staggered, and would have dropped the baby, had not Diane leaped across the floor and caught her, taking the baby from her arms.

The woman's face was pallid, but she managed a wan smile, gasped: "It—it's nothing. Just a flesh wound in the arm!"

Diane led her upstairs, with the aid of another woman.

Bullets were coming thick and fast now, spattering into all four walls of the building. The women were replying to the fire of the Uhlans, shooting as rapidly as possible with their anti-quated rifles.

The thing had come so suddenly that many of them were dazed, not realizing the full extent of the calamity that had struck them. They had known, of course, that discovery by a passing patrol might come at any day—but they had hoped that they would escape notice. Now they were discovered, and they knew in their hearts that they could not for long defy the whole might of the Central Empire. The only thing they could look forward to was to die fighting, with their children, rather than be captured and subjected to the indignities for which these Uhlans were notorious.

The room quickly became thick with smoke, and the air became heavy. There were twenty women at the windows and loopholes, firing with soldierly regularity, and there were others in the rear rooms.

Mrs. Martinson had taken command, and she was urging the women not to waste any ammunition. "We'll need every round, girls," she warned. "And we better save the last bullets for ourselves. For my part, I swear I won't be taken alive by those devils!"

Tim Donovan had picked up one of the spare rifles, and he went to one of the loopholes in the wall, alongside the door. He could see the Uhlans down on the dirt road. They had taken cover behind trees, and were firing methodically, while another group on the other side of the road was hauling a huge dead tree trunk from the field on the opposite side.

Mrs. Martinson's voice came over his shoulder. "What in the world do you think they're going to do with that?"

"They're going to make a battering ram," Tim told her moodily. "They'll smash down the door. They don't intend to waste much time here!"

"A battering ram! But good God, how will they get close enough to use it? We could shoot them down—"

"Not when they're ready, Mrs. Martinson. They'll send a hail of lead in here, that will drive everyone from the loopholes and windows. Under cover of that barrage, they'll come up close to the door."

THE ROOM was filled with the thunderous sound of rifle fire, and the air was full of smoke and burnt powder. A girl of eleven was carrying water to the women. So far, the enemy's fire had not succeeded in penetrating the walls of the house, nor in piercing the obstructions placed across the windows.

But a whining carbine slug whistled through one of the loopholes, struck a woman in the eye, killing her instantly.

Mrs. Martinson groaned. "That's Lillian White. I've known her since we were kids!"

A woman came in from the kitchen to report that the enemy troopers were tearing down part of the barn. "We got a couple of them, but they moved around to the other side of the barn. They seem to be pulling boards out of the barn wall."

Tim Donovan nodded. "That's to make a shield for the men who will operate the battering ram!"

He was right. In a few minutes, several of the Uhlans appeared in the road, carrying a huge wooden shield. They began lugging it over toward where the battering ram was lying ready and Tim said grimly: "It's about time to call that off!"

He raised the rifle to his shoulder, sighted through the loop-hole, and fired five times in quick succession.

His training with Operator 5 had not been wasted. He dropped five of the troopers, and the others retreated hastily, away from the battering ram, deserting their wooden shield in the middle of the road.

"Good shot!" Mrs. Martinson praised. "That ought to hold them for a while!"

But the continuous barrage from all four sides of the house did not diminish. The Uhlans kept up a steady fire, and often their slugs whistled through the loopholes. The casualties within the house increased alarmingly. Diane was kept busy upstairs, tending the wounded.

For three hours the enemy continued to pour lead into the building, and the women answered, rapidly diminishing their store of ammunition.

DRUMS OF DESTRUCTION

Mrs. Martinson was everywhere at once, organizing shifts at the loopholes, assigning others to the kitchen to prepare food, seeing to it that the wounded were taken upstairs.

Tim continued at his station at the loophole. Three times he kept the Uhlans from reaching their shield and battering ram, and as a result, the full force of the troopers' fire was directed at his loophole. A shot grazed his cheek, and another struck the stock of his rifle, but he remained fortunately unwounded.

Toward evening, Mrs. Martinson came over to him. "What are we going to do tonight?" she asked. "When it gets dark, we won't be able to keep them away. They can steal up under cover of darkness, and smash in the door!"

Tim nodded. "I was thinking of that. The only answer is that someone must go for help."

"But where could we get help? We're in the midst of the enemy country—"

"John Mooney has several hundred men," Tim told her. "If he could be reached, there's a chance. By morning, if they haven't sacked the house, there'll be so many troopers here that it'll take a small army to raise the siege. Someone must try to run the gauntlet of the Uhlans and get out to look for John Mooney!"

A voice behind him said tightly: "I'll do it, Tim!"

DIANE ELLIOT had come downstairs in time to hear, above the crackling of the rifle fire, what he said. Her blouse was spotted with red, where the blood of her wounded patients had spilled on it. Her face was drawn and pale from the sight of the suffering and death upstairs. But she carried herself with courage and poise.

"I'll go, Mrs. Martinson," she went on. "I've got to get out anyway. There are still a half dozen local leaders to warn. If I don't see them, they won't be at the rendezvous at the zero hour on Wednesday, and Operator 5's plan of attack will fall through."

"Me, too, Di," Tim Donovan added. "We've each got six men to see between now and Wednesday morning. I'm going through those Uhlans with you."

Mrs. Martinson protested. "But how on earth can you do it? They're surrounding the house. The minute you show yourselves, you'll be shot down."

"We'll have to chance that," Diane Elliot said simply. "Operator 5 is relying on us to carry his message, and we can't let him down!"

"But suppose you're killed getting away from here," the big woman insisted. "Your messages would still not be delivered."

"We'll take care of that!" Diane decided. She produced paper and pencil, and swiftly wrote the names of the men, leaders of the civilian groups in the Occupied Territory, whom she was to see. After each name she wrote the place where she was to meet the man.

Then she handed the paper to Tim Donovan, and he did the same. They had both committed those names and places to memory, so as not to betray the men in the event that either of them should be captured.

When he was finished, Tim handed the paper to Mrs. Martinson.

Diane spoke to her earnestly. "Keep that, Mrs. Martinson, and guard it with your life. If we should be killed getting out of here, ask for two volunteers from among the women here. Let them go out to contact those men. I've written down what they're to tell those men—the places where they are to mobilize, behind the enemy lines. The zero hour is six-thirty, Wednesday. If we're killed, I leave it to you to carry on for us!"

"But how will I know what has happened to you?" Mrs. Martinson demanded. "Suppose something happens to you after you get out of sight—"

"You'll know we got through, if help comes for you. Because the first thing we'll do is to try to find John Mooney. If we get past these Uhlans, you can depend on us not to leave you here to the mercy of the enemy!"

"All right," Mrs. Martinson agreed reluctantly. "But how do you expect to get through? Will you wait till dark—"

"No!" Tim told her. "We're going now! The sooner we get hold of John Mooney, the better will be your chances of getting out of this farmhouse alive!"

"But how—"

Tim motioned to the loophole. "See that clump of trees where the Uhlans' horses are tethered? There's only one man guarding those horses. If we can get across the open ground between here and the road, we can seize a couple of mounts and be off before the troopers know what it's all about."

"But you'd be riddled with bullets before you got to the road—"

"That's where *you* come in, Mrs. Martinson," Tim told her. "I want you to station your women at every available loophole and window here in the front. Leave only enough women at the rear of the house to show the Uhlans they're still there. Then, when Diane and I are ready to go, your women will open up with their rifles, and keep the road swept clear. Let them keep on firing until we reach the horses—"

"But if only a single shot from one of the troopers hits you—"

Tim smiled grimly. "Those are the chances of war, Mrs. Martinson. Now, give your orders!"

The big woman sighed. "If I were only forty pounds lighter, I'd insist on going with you!" She moved away to shift the women from the rear of the house to the front.

Tim and Diane went upstairs for a moment, and said goodbye to little Johnny and Marie Mooney.

Marie clung to Diane's hands. "If you see our mama," she begged, *"please* tell her to come to us quickly. We want our mama!"

Diane kissed both children, keeping back the tears by an effort of will. "Be good, children, and I'll send your daddy to you!"

Then she swiftly turned away, gripped Tim's arm, and ran with him downstairs. Everything was set down below. Two women were at the door, ready to remove the huge iron bar and swing it open. Some fifty women were stationed around the walls at the loopholes, ready to open fire. Diane took Tim's hand in hers, pressed it hard. "Here's where we part, Timmy. May God be with you!"

"And with you, too, Di!" the lad said huskily.

Diane turned to Mrs. Martinson. "We're ready!" she announced.

CHAPTER 6
THE BLACK HOLE OF KANSAS

IT HAD been Jimmy Christopher's original intention, when he set out after the Battle of Medicine Bow, to allow himself to be captured close behind the enemy lines. But the sight of Captain Storm and his Wyoming Riflemen, attired in the uniforms of the dead soldiers of the Purple Empire, gave him another, and a better idea.

Captain Storm had taken the uniform of the Major of Purple Infantry, and he looked and acted the part to perfection. They had succeeded in capturing alive more than a hundred of the Purple Troopers, and the uniforms of these men were unmarred by bullet holes. In addition, they found close to seventy dead Purple soldiers whose clothes were also fit to be used. Thus, they were able to march into enemy territory with almost a hundred and seventy men.

Jimmy Christopher knew that he would have difficulty in getting far into enemy territory attired as an American officer; while if he dressed as a civilian he might be arrested or shot by any roving patrols of the Purple armies, but the chances were that they would not bother to search him, in which case they would not find the false dispatches.

He therefore conceived the idea of having himself taken into custody at once by Captain Storm and his hundred and seventy bogus troopers, and marched directly toward Purple Headquarters.

When he broached the idea to Colonel Smithfield and

Captain Storm, they both shouted aloud in their enthusiasm. It was the perfect set-up.

"You see," Jimmy explained, "we could march deep into Kansas, with me as your prisoner. There's an Intelligence unit of the Purple Army at Phillipsburg. We could ride there, and

RUDOLPH

FLEXNER

KREMER

you could turn me over to the Intelligence officer there. As soon as he reads the dispatch, he'll communicate by heliograph or carrier pigeon with their headquarters at Topeka. Marshal Kremer will either fall for those dispatches, or he won't. If he doesn't fall, then we just didn't make the grade. But if he does, he'll immediately countermand his orders to move the reserves north from Pueblo. He'll keep them down there. Then, after the Intelligence officer has sent his message, you can raid the guard house and take me out!"

"It sounds perfect," Captain Storm admitted. "But I don't

like the idea of your taking the risk. They might shoot you out of hand—"

"It'll be your job to see that they don't," Jimmy Christopher grinned.

At the last minute, as the troop was ready to start on its adventure, a heliograph message came in from General Hank Sheridan. The news of the victory in the pass had already been communicated to him, and his message, after it was transcribed, read:

> OPERATOR 5... HAVE BEEN IN COMMUNICA-TION WITH Z-7 AT GHQ IN SALT LAKE CITY... HE INSTRUCTS ME TO CONGRATULATE YOU ON VICTORY BUT HE ABSOLUTELY FORBIDS YOU TO CARRY OUT OTHER PLAN... HE FORBIDS YOU TO CROSS ENEMY LINES... YOU ARE TO ASK FOR A VOLUNTEER TO TAKE YOUR PLACE... PLEASE OBEY THIS ORDER... SHERIDAN*

* AUTHOR'S NOTE: Z-7, it will be recalled, had been the head of the United States Intelligence Service. It was under him that Operator 5 worked. A strange, reticent man of great dynamic ability, he had backed up every move made by Operator 5. After the death of the last president of the United States, Z-7 had become the unofficial ruler of that portion of the country which was not under Purple domination. And now, though he was the titular Commander-in-Chief of the American Defense Force, he left the actual business of military strategy to General Sheridan and Operator 5. He himself devoted his time to the task of coördinating the all-too-few resources of the west coast, to keeping peace and harmony among the few Western

DRUMS OF DESTRUCTION

One of Colonel Smithfield's cavalrymen had taken the message over the heliograph, and it was Smithfield himself who handed it to Jimmy Christopher.

"Too bad, Operator 5," the colonel said. "I guess you can't go—"

Operator 5 took the message from him, and tore it to shreds.

"Forget you ever got this, Colonel," he said tensely. "I want to make sure that Kremer is taken in by the dispatches, and I can't trust anyone else to do the job the way I want the job done. I want to be on the spot myself when those dispatches are turned over to the enemy!"

At last Jimmy Christopher prevailed. Colonel Smithfield shrugged.

"Okay," he conceded. "I can't stop you. My men swear by you. I think they'd defy me if it came to the question of arresting you. So go ahead, and God bless you!"

States which remained free of the Purple yoke. Z-7 had seen Jimmy Christopher enter the Intelligence Service as a youth, and had seen him develop until he was the ace operator of the Service. He loved Jimmy almost as a son, and it could be readily understood that he would not want him to risk his life in this venture. Historians, looking back upon this incident, are wont to blame Z-7 for not having insisted more drastically upon having Operator 5 refrain from going. But those who criticize Z-7 forget that the Intelligence Chief had no real authority to stop Operator 5 from going. Historians also agree that it was a foolhardy thing for Operator 5 to do, in view of the fact that his ability was so necessary to the American cause; but in the light of later events it proved to have been the right course of action.

Jimmy Christopher shook hands with him, and mounted his horse. Captain Storm gave the signal, and his company of one hundred and seventy bogus Purple troops swung onto their mounts. Each man led an extra horse to be used as a remount. They had borrowed them from the Oregon Cavalry, and they had chosen the best, for upon the speed of their horses might hang the life of every man in the troop if their disguise should be pierced.

The bugle sounded, and they set off through Willow Creek Pass.

Jimmy Christopher rode in the lead, alongside Captain Storm, who wore the major's uniform with all the aplomb of a haughty officer of the Central Empire.

Operator 5 had taken the revolver from his holster and stuck it in his waistband, under his tunic, so that if they met any Central Empire troops, he would appear to be truly a prisoner.

It was thus that they rode into the enemy territory, swarming with Rudolph's troopers.*

---

* AUTHOR'S NOTE: Military writers generally concede that this foray into enemy territory of Storm's Wyoming Riflemen was the most daring undertaking of the war. Consider that here were a hundred and seventy-one men, disguised as enemy troopers, riding into the heart of the enemy territory during war time, without so much as a marching order to show to any superior officer whom they might encounter. Consider also that they would be consistently marching *away from* instead of toward the front lines, and thus would make themselves doubly liable to questioning and suspicion; and consider that in the event of discovery they would be marooned in hostile

DRUMS OF DESTRUCTION

THEY RODE swiftly, so as to avoid the enemy reinforcements which the pilot had reported to be coming around the north side of Chambers Lake. Those reinforcements would arrive only to face Colonel Smithfield's men dug into the very trenches which Purple troops had occupied only a few hours before. Willow Creek Pass would be once more closed to the Purple Army.

And in the meantime, Operator 5 and his hundred and seventy genial captors crossed north of the Rocky Mountain National Park, and started on the first leg of their historic adventure.

The first test of their Purple disguises came when they were a little south of Fort Collins. The town had been razed to the ground, as had hundreds of others in this territory, and a regiment of South-European Infantry was encamped on a narrow plateau just off the road.

Sentries were patrolling the road, and they could see regimental headquarters, with the flag of the Purple Empire above it. A lieutenant rode out to meet them, and Storm raised his hand in signal for the company to halt. The Wyoming men closed up their ranks, sitting stiffly on their mounts, like ramrods, in the fashion of the Purple cavalry.

country, surrounded by countless divisions of trained troops against whom they could hope to do little but go down fighting. As the great historian, Stievers, has said in his monumental *The History of the Purple War,* the adventure was "foolhardy in the extreme, but prone to success through the very incredibility of its foolhardiness!"

The Purple lieutenant saluted stiffly, and said to Storm: "Colonel Moltke presents his compliments, and wishes to know what is the news from the front lines." He glanced curiously at Jimmy Christopher, who sat alongside Captain Storm, his eyes resting significantly on Jimmy's empty holster.

Storm replied: "Present to Colonel Moltke the respects of Major von Krumpert. Our troops did not succeed in holding Willow Creek Pass, and the enemy is once more in possession. But we have made prisoner a very important American courier, whom we are escorting to headquarters. I regret that I cannot stop to pay my respects in person to Colonel Moltke, but time presses."

The lieutenant nodded. "I understand, sir. I shall give your message to the Colonel. Thank you for the news."

He saluted, and moved out of the road, allowing the company to pass. When they were well out of sight of the enemy regiment, Storm breathed a sigh of relief. "Boy!" he exclaimed, "I made it! That lieutenant thought I was the real goods!" Jimmy Christopher smiled. Storm's accent was not the pure accent of the Purple language. But there were so many different nationalities under the flag of the Central Empire, and one encountered so many different accents in the Purple armies, that Storm had passed with flying colors.

Now they rode swiftly eastward, not sparing their horses. At Fort Morgan they found a remount station of the Purple Army, and secured fresh horses, Captain Storm signing a requisition for them in the name of Major von Krumpert. He had ascertained the name of the dead major whom he was impersonating, by questioning the captured troopers at Willow Creek Pass, and he knew all about the man.

Their only danger was in meeting some other officer who might be personally acquainted with Major Krumpert. In that case their only recourse would be to fight it out. They secured the horses without question, however, and rode on. They decided that hereafter, if they should meet other Purple detachments, Storm would give some fictitious name instead of that of von Krumpert.

IT WAS toward late afternoon that they crossed the Colorado-Kansas border, and an hour later that they spied the solitary rider heading in their direction for down the road. The sun was in the man's eyes, so that he had not seen them yet, and Jimmy Christopher said: "Let's get off the road and waylay this man. He may be a Purple courier."

Storm nodded, and ordered the company to separate, taking cover on both sides of the road. The rider seemed to be in desperate, frantic haste. He looked neither to the right nor the left, urging his mount continuously forward. But just then one of the horses in Storm's company whinnied, and they could see that the rider had heard it.

The man pulled his horse up short, kicking up a small gale of dust. He sat suddenly motionless, watchful.

Jimmy Christopher, standing beside Storm, frowned and said: "That's funny. Why should a Purple Empire rider stop so suspiciously when he hears a horse whinny? He shouldn't expect to meet American troops—"

The rider was advancing again, cautiously, a hand on the gun in his holster. From this distance he seemed to be rather small, and wiry. And he was not in the Purple uniform. As he drew closer, Jimmy Christopher tautened, and gripped Storm's arm.

"It's Tim Donovan!" he gasped.

He swung up on his horse, pushed out from behind the clump of trees where they had taken cover, with Storm close behind. The other Wyoming men, seeing Storm and Jimmy come into the open, followed their example.

And Tim Donovan suddenly swung his mount around, began to race away from them. The distance between them was small now and Jimmy Christopher shouted: "Tim! Tim! Come back here!"

At the sound of his voice, Tim Donovan slowed up, came to a halt. He turned, still doubtful, still with his hand on the revolver.

"It's all right, Tim!" Jimmy shouted. "These aren't Purple troops."

Tim Donovan let out a whoop of joy, and raced to meet them. He pulled his horse up close to Operator 5's, and reached out a hand.

"Gosh, Jimmy, it's good to see you!" The lad's eyes expressed the depth of his emotion. "I thought I was a goner, seeing all these Purple uniforms. I never expected to see *you* here!"

Swiftly, Jimmy explained their mission. "And now, how come you're in this neck of the woods?" he demanded. "According to your instructions, you should be heading northeast—"

"Wait, Jimmy. I've got some bad news for you! Diane and I have just run the gauntlet of a company of Purple Uhlans, who are attacking the Martinson Farm, not two miles from here. There are almost two hundred women and children in the farmhouse!"

Almost incoherently, he related the events of the day, telling how he and Diane had met John Mooney, and how they had subsequently found themselves besieged in the huge Martinson Farm.

"Which way?" Jimmy Christopher demanded tersely.

Tim pointed a shaking finger. "Down this road."

Jimmy Christopher glanced at Captain Storm. "It's damned important for us to get these dispatches into Kremer's hands. But we can't let those women and children die."

Captain Storm met his gaze squarely. "The decision is yours, Operator 5. You are in command. My troop is at your disposal—but naturally, my personal instinct would be to go to the aid of those people."

Jimmy nodded. "That's what we're going to do!" he said softly. Then his voice crackled. "Let's ride!"

With a shout, the troop swung into a canter. The men unslung their carbines, preparing for action.

TIM RODE between Jimmy and Captain Storm. Behind them the drumming of a hundred and seventy horses' hooves made martial music on the road. They had left their spare mounts with a guard, in order not to be hampered. And the company of Wyoming riflemen itched to come to grips with the Uhlans who had hitherto violated, tortured and killed American women in the Occupied Territory.

Tim shouted over to Operator 5: "I was trying to locate John Mooney, to get him to ride to Martinson's Farm. But he must have started for the rendezvous already. If I hadn't met you, I don't know what I'd have done!"

The sun was disappearing fast at their backs. As they rode, Operator 5 caught sight of a plume of smoke about a mile away. The smoke spread, becoming a thick blanket, flecked with flame.

Tim Donovan saw it too, and he exclaimed: "God, they've set fire to the wheat! I was afraid they'd think of that. If the fire reaches the house, it'll drive all those women and children out into the open!"

Jimmy Christopher's face hardened, and his mouth drew into a thin line. Almost instinctively he spurred his horse to a faster pace. Behind him, the troop of riflemen also saw the flame and smoke, and they guessed what it meant.

Now they could see the farmhouse, and could distinguish the figures of the mounted Uhlans waiting with drawn sabers in the clearing between the building and the road.

The fire had jumped from the wheat field to the house itself, and the dry shingles of the roof were burning intensely.

"God!" Captain Storm shouted, "those women will be burned alive!"

Even as he spoke, the front door of the farmhouse was thrust open, and the unfortunate women came streaming out. Flames began pouring from the windows, and the roof started to cave in. They had remained inside until the last possible moment; and now they were coming out to fight in the open with clubbed rifles against the gleaming bayonets and the slashing sabers of the Uhlans.

Jimmy Christopher kept his eyes on that dreadful scene, and

bent low over his horse's mane, urging it to the last ounce of its endurance, Tim Donovan and Captain Storm kept pace with him, while the Wyoming riflemen crowded close at their heels.

Ahead of them a scene of mad slaughter was taking place such as has never been recorded in history since the Black Hole of Calcutta.

The Uhlans raced their horses at the almost defenseless women, cutting them down mercilessly with wide sweeps of their sabers, or driving the points of their bayonets into the women's breasts. Women and children perished there before the very eyes of the racing Wyoming men, while they pushed their horses to the limit to reach the spot before the carnage should be finished.

The fire within the farmhouse was converting the building into a blazing furnace, and the last of the occupants were crowding out of it, only to meet the choice of dying upon the bayonets of the Uhlans, or of going back into that flaming inferno.

The Uhlans crowding in from the other sides of the house to take place in the sport saw Jimmy Christopher's racing troop, but evidently thought they were Central Empire troopers coming to join the grisly fun. They continued with the bloody work almost until the moment when Operator 5 and his men came abreast of them on the road.

The clearing in front of the house was gruesome with the dead and bloody bodies of the victims, while the surviving women were attempting frantically to protect their children from the vicious thrusts of the bayonets. In one fleeting glimpse Jimmy Christopher saw a woman fling herself between a trooper and a child that the man had been about to impale; saw the woman take the full length of the bayonet's gleaming steel in her bosom, and saw the trooper callously disengage his foot from the stirrup to kick the woman's body off his bayonet.

And then they were close to the fracas.

In a hoarse voice, clouded with rage, Operator 5 shouted: "Charge!"

And the troop of Wyoming riflemen, with sabers flashing in the air, thundered down like an avenging avalanche of wrath upon the Uhlans.

THE PURPLE troopers did not realize that they were being attacked until Operator 5, Tim Donovan and Captain Storm were in on them, firing point-blank. Then the first wave of the Wyoming riflemen catapulted into the Uhlans, and the Purple soldiers uttered shouts of mingled surprise and consternation.

They swung from their comparatively harmless sport of killing virtually defenseless women and children, to the grim business of fighting for their lives against a company of Americans maddened by the things they had just seen done to American women.

There was a full squadron of Uhlans, numbering two hundred and fifty, against the hundred and seventy Americans. But from the very first clash of sabers there was no question of numerical superiority. The Americans attacked as if they were ten times their number, fighting an irresistible, madly reckless sort of battle that the Uhlans could not hope to match.

They went down by the dozen before the wild onslaught, while the women cheered hysterically.

And then suddenly the Uhlans broke. They turned, slapping their horses, and fled from the wrath of the Wyoming riflemen. The Americans set off after them, cutting them down as they fled, and heedless of cries for mercy, cries of *"Kamerad"*—heeding nothing but the gruesome fact that some fifty women and children lay dead there in front of the flaming house.

Far out into the road they pursued the fleeing Uhlans, and hardly forty of the original two hundred and fifty escaped.

At last the Americans began to spur back toward the farmhouse, their anger gone, picking their way among the dead bodies of the troopers in the road. Their hearts were heavy with grief, for they knew that many American men would not sleep tonight, seeing before them the images of murdered wives, daughters, mothers.

The farmhouse was blazing furiously.

Tim Donovan had dragged Jimmy Christopher into the flaming building, shouting to him above the din of the battle: "There's a woman upstairs that's giving birth to a baby. We got to get her out!"

Operator 5 followed the boy in through the flames, shielding his face with his uniform tunic. The boy ripped the tunic from a dead Uhlan and did the same. They worked their way up the stairs, groped through falling timbers to the far corner where Tim had last seen Mrs. Slocum.

He found her there, struggling up from the bed, while beside her sat Mrs. Martinson, holding a pulsing bit of newborn humanity. Mrs. Martinson had stayed with the expectant mother. And through the turmoil of the battle below, through

The Uhlans cut them down with sweeping sabers....

the inferno of fire and of falling roof, she had helped another boy into the world!

Now they had thought themselves trapped in the fire, and

Mrs. Martinson had been about to throw the infant from the window rather than let it be consumed by the flames. Both women were almost unconscious when Tim and Jimmy Christopher made their appearance.

Mrs. Martinson uttered a glad shout, and held out the heavily-swathed infant to Tim Donovan, who took it, covered it with his tunic, and ran like a quarterback with a ball, through the flames toward the stairs.

Mrs. Martinson staggered to her feet and followed, and

Jimmy Christopher bent to the bed, wrapped a heavy blanket about Mrs. Slocum, then raised her in his arms, carried her through the flames.

The fire licked at his face, at his clothes, but he managed to come through, reached the stairs just as the whole roof, rumbling like a wounded elephant, came down with a crash. He escaped the falling timbers by a hair's breadth, and reached the ground floor, sprang through the open door and out into the clearing where a dozen willing hands took his burden, laid her on blankets on the ground.

They placed the new-born boy beside her, and the mother smiled, a smile that was ineffably beautiful, like the smile of a madonna.

"Pray God he never sees a war when he grows up!" she murmured.

And Operator 5, his eyes bleak, whispered: "Amen!"

CHAPTER 7
THE FALSE TRAIL

AND NOW, Operator 5 and Captain Storm were faced with a serious dilemma. Those Uhlans who had escaped would no doubt report the presence of a body of Americans wearing Purple uniforms. They would also report the fact that an American officer had accompanied them. Thus, Jimmy Christopher's plan to have himself turned over to the Intelligence Department of the Purple Empire must now go by the board.

Captain Storm set out sentries a half mile up each end of the road, to warn of the approach of an enemy, while the Wyoming men aided the surviving women to tend the wounded and bury their dead.

The scene was one that will never be forgotten as long as Americans live.*

The farmhouse itself was now nothing but a heap of charred logs and cinders, from which the smoke still curled up in little spurts. In the clearing, first aid was being given to eight or nine women and to two of the riflemen who had been wounded in the battle. These unfortunates were made as comfortable as possible on army blankets, folded on the cold ground. Night had set in, and the men were compelled to work by the light of several bonfires. On the west side of the house, fifteen or twenty men were engaged in the grim task of digging graves for the dead. Operator 5, Tim Donovan, Diane Elliot and Captain Storm were gathered near the road, in a bitter council of war.

Storm was gloomily despondent. "We have a hundred and twenty surviving women and children here," he said, "some of them wounded. We've got to get them out of the Occupied Territory, together with the wounded. How are we going to do

---

* Author's Note: This scene, as well as the scene of the slaughter of the women when they ran from the burning house, has been immortalized by the renowned American artist, Howland Gardner, in his two great canvasses— one entitled, "Slaughter," and the other, "After the Battle." Both these immortal canvasses now hang on a special wall in the White House, as mute testimony to the peril of unpreparedness.

that, through hostile country, with the whole Purple Army on the lookout for us?"

Jimmy Christopher's eyes were bleak. "We'll have to do it somehow, Captain. We've sent for the reserve mounts. We can rig up palanquins for the wounded, and the other women will have to ride the extra mounts, carrying their children. You and your troop will escort them across to Willow Creek Pass, and get them through the Purple lines somehow."

"And what about the dispatches?" Storm asked. "How will you get them into Kremer's hands? You've got to work fast now. Tomorrow is Tuesday, and that'll leave only a day and a half before zero hour."

"We'll have to go back to my original plan," Jimmy decided. "I'll get myself captured, so that the dispatches can be found on me. I'll have to chance their shooting me on sight."

He raised a hand, as Storm, Diane and Tim all began to protest at the same time. "I'm in command," he said sternly, "and it's going to be done the way I say. I don't know why you're all so careful of me. You, Diane, and Tim, will be taking just as much of a risk. You're to go on, both of you, visiting your list of local leaders. As soon as you've completed the rounds, you'll head back to Willow Creek Pass. The three of us will meet just this side of the pass—" he produced paper and pencil, and drew a rough sketch from memory, of the country around Willow Creek Pass—"right here. It's a bit of wooded country, and we can hide out in case the enemy is present. I'll want to see you both, to get your reports. I've got to know how many volunteers are going to support our attack from behind the enemy lines."

Diane and Tim studied the map carefully, marking in their memory the exact location of the spot Jimmy had indicated. Then he destroyed the sheet of paper. "We'll wait no later than three o'clock Wednesday afternoon, for each other. Whoever doesn't show up by then—why, we won't expect him anymore."

Jimmy Christopher took Diane Elliot in his arms, held her close. For an instant, his lips brushed hers. "Goodbye, darling," he whispered. "There's a very good chance that at least one of us won't come back to the meeting place. In any case, will you remember—that I love you?"

Her eyes were moist as she raised them to his. "I'll remember, Jimmy—always. And if it should be I who doesn't come back, think of me sometimes, darling!"

Jimmy swallowed hard, turned away from her and gripped Tim Donovan's hand. "Go to it, Tim," he said huskily. "And try hard to come through. Now—the two of you—on your way!"

He watched, immovably, while Tim and Diane selected horses and mounted. Diane rode north, while Tim had to head east—

East toward Council Grove ultimately, where the following day was destined to see him a prisoner of the Emperor, sentenced to be shot at sunrise, with Operator 5's sacrifice the price of his life.

IT WAS well on into the night when the burial of the slaughtered women and children was concluded. Strangely, no Purple troops came to disturb the solemn moment when every one of the Wyoming riflemen stood at attention, and Jimmy Christopher recited a simple service over the pitiful graves.

Perhaps the fleeing Uhlans had not been able to get up enough courage to report their defeat; or perhaps they had not yet been able to contact a large enough body of enemy troops to attack the Americans. In any event, Operator 5 and Captain Storm made their arrangements undisturbed, and the troop finally started west, convoying the women, the children, and the wounded.

Jimmy Christopher took leave of them, and pushed further east in search of Purple troops to capture him.

He followed virtually in the steps of Tim Donovan for the first few miles, heading toward Phillipsburg, where he knew that there was an enemy Intelligence office. He was forced several times to conceal himself off the road, while detachment of Purple troopers passed, riding west. The enemy were patrolling the roads heavily now—which meant that they must by this time have received news of the fight at Martinson's farm.

From his knowledge of Rudolph's character, Jimmy Christopher was sure that the Emperor would leave no stone unturned to effect the capture of that daring troop of Wyoming riflemen who had raided Purple territory and had inflicted such heavy losses on the Uhlans. Every road would be patrolled, every possible means of reaching the American lines watched. Storm would be lucky if he got through with his charges without a fight. And that added watchfulness on the part of the enemy would make the tasks of Diane and Tim doubly difficult.

He rode on into the night, wondering whether they were still free. The dispatches which he was carrying had been carefully prepared. They purported to be a resume of the plans of the American Defense Force for a drive against the enemy positions in the Continental Divide at Concha Pass, and it was quite natural that the Americans should ask the help of those civilians in the Occupied Territory who were willing to risk their lives. The dispatches further contained false orders, which would lead Rudolph and Kremer to believe that the civilians were to gather at a spot far removed from Canon City, where they were really being ordered to meet by Diane and Tim. If those dispatches could only be gotten into competent enemy hands before morning.

Thus preoccupied, Operator 5 reined his horse around a bend in the road, and brought up sharp. A man stood in the road, examining the right hind shoe of his horse, with the aid of a flashlight. The man was attired in the uniform of a staff major of the Purple Army, and he was cursing under his breath. The horse had evidently cast a shoe.

The staff major straightened from his inspection of the horse, and swung his flashlight up to cover Operator 5. He began: "I need a horse—" and broke off with a sharp gasp as he glimpsed the American uniform of Jimmy Christopher. "An American!" he shouted, and reached for his gun.

Jimmy Christopher's eyes were narrowed. Here was a perfect chance to carry out his plan. Who was better for the purpose than a staff major? If he gave himself up and allowed himself to be searched, the major would find the papers, understand their importance, and at once turn them over to Purple Headquarters.

The major's gun was halfway out of its holster.

"I surrender!" Operator 5 said, with just the right amount of fear in his voice to make it convincing.

"Surrender!" the major grunted. "I can't be bothered with prisoners tonight. You must die now, American!"

He raised the gun.

In an instant, the imminent failure of his plan loomed in the mind of Operator 5. This major was in a hurry. He wanted a horse and nothing else. He had heard of the American raiders at the Martinson Farm, assumed that this was one of them.

He was interested in getting a horse, and nothing else. He would shoot Operator 5, leave him in the road without touching him, and ride away with his commandeered horse. The dispatches would remain undiscovered....

ALL THIS flashed through Jimmy Christopher's mind while the staff officer was raising his gun. And Jimmy's mind flashed the impulse to his muscles. His hand had been under the tunic, gripping the butt of his gun. Now it streaked out, and the gun flashed flame barely a split second after the major's gun.

Jimmy had pulled sharply on the reins to the left, and his horse shied over in that direction almost before he fired. The major's bullet went wide, and his own slug caught the staff officer between the eyes. The man's arms went out in a peculiar, stiff motion, he seemed to rise up on his toes as if reaching for the sky, and then he toppled over. His horse reared up, then pawed the ground, and wheeled, started to run wildly across the fields. In a moment it had disappeared. Operator 5 was left alone in the night with the dead staff major.

Bitterly, he dismounted and approached the other. He had

thought that here his self-inflicted sacrifice was to end. But the man's natural callousness had lost him his life, and postponed the execution of Operator 5's plan. Had the staff major been content to accept surrender of the unknown American instead of shooting him down, he might be alive at this moment.

Jimmy Christopher raised his head sharply as he heard other hoof beats on the road. He listened intently for a moment, then got down to his knees, lowered his ear to the ground. He judged that there were fifteen or twenty horsemen coming in his direction from the east. They were not riding fast, and they must be a half mile or so away. Probably a patrol.

And suddenly, Jimmy Christopher's eyes gleamed with inspiration. Here was opportunity such as he had not hoped for!

Feverishly he stripped off his tunic, and then knelt beside the dead major. The body was inert, heavy, and clumsy to move about. But he managed to get the major's uniform jacket off, and to slip his own tunic on to the dead man's body. He buttoned it up, placed his own cap beside the corpse, and then donned the uniform jacket of the major. He looked around in the dark until he found the Purple officer's helmet, and put that on, too. The Purple patrol was approaching closer and closer, and there was only a matter of minutes left before they would arrive. Jimmy remembered the identity disk around the major's throat, and he opened the tunic at the neck, snapped the thin chain that held it, and slipped the disk into his pocket. He went through the pockets of the major's breeches to make sure there was nothing in them to identify him, and then he stood up just as the Purple patrol came into sight.

They were still far down the road, but the powerful flashlights they carried bathed Jimmy and the dead man in light.

Operator 5 raised his arm, waved to them, and he heard a low-voiced command, saw the patrol swing into the double quick. They reached him in a moment, and a sergeant dismounted, saluted Jimmy respectfully, looking at the epaulets on his shoulder.

"Sergeant Zippert, *Herr* Major," he said, "in charge of Kansas Province Military Patrol Number Nineteen. You have killed an American, I see."

Jimmy Christopher nodded. "My horse cast a shoe," he lied, "and as I was examining it, this American rode up. We both fired at once, and I killed him. My horse became frightened and ran away."

"May I congratulate you, *Herr* Major," the sergeant said. "This must be one of those *verdammte* Americans from the raiding party that we are searching for."

"Let's see who he is," Jimmy said, and knelt beside the dead body. He thrust his hand inside the tunic, drew out the false dispatches which he had left there. He opened them, while the sergeant lent him the light of his flash.

Jimmy pretended to read for a moment, and then whistled. "This is far more important than I thought, Sergeant. This man is carrying dispatches from the American Defense Force, which outline their whole plan of campaign. It seems that they are planning something wholly unexpected. These dispatches should be turned over to headquarters at once!"

"I suppose you will take them, *Herr Major?*"

"No, I cannot. I am on an important mission of my own. You will have to ride fast to headquarters with your patrol, Sergeant. You have my permission to go. Everything depends on these dispatches, reaching headquarters. You understand?"

"I understand, sir. I shall tell them how you killed the American. And may I know your name, sir?"

Jimmy gave the first name that entered his head, and impatiently waved the sergeant toward his horse. "Hurry, Sergeant. There is not a moment to be lost!"

He stood in the road watching the patrol disappear toward the east bearing those dispatches. At last, he had succeeded. Kremer would have the false information by blinker lights within an hour, and if he believed them, he would order his reserves to remain at Pueblo instead of moving north. Everything now depended on Kremer's gullibility.

Jimmy sighed. His task so far was completed. There was nothing further that he could do.

He decided to retain the major's uniform as an aid to getting through the front lines. But he knelt beside the dead body once more, and removed his own tunic and cap from the corpse, making a bundle of it. He would take that along too. He moved the body over into the ditch alongside the road, and covered it with dead branches and leaves. It was the best grave he could provide for the major at this time.

Then he mounted his horse and set off toward the west. He was through. But how, he wondered, were Diane and Tim making out?

HE WAS to learn in good time. His uniform got him through

91

to the front lines without hindrance, and there, early the following morning, as he pushed through the mountainous country north of Willow Creek Pass, he caught the sound of continuous rifle fire. His horse was jaded, and he was weary, for it was Tuesday morning, and he had not slept since Sunday. His eyes were heavy and red-rimmed. But his body was alert, his mind keen, as he reined in his horse on a rise in the road that gave him a view of the country for miles to the southeast, as far as the foothills of the Medicine Bow Range.

From where he sat, he could see Willow Creek Pass, and the copse of woods where he had instructed Storm and Diane and Tim to meet him.

His pulse beat faster as he saw the thick masses of Purple Infantry surrounding a small company of cavalry. At this distance it was difficult to distinguish friend from foe, but Jimmy, watching carefully, saw many female figures among those in the surrounded detachment.

That would be Captain Storm's troop of Wyoming riflemen. Apparently they had ridden into an enemy trap, when they were within sight of safety. The riflemen had dismounted and formed a hollow square, in the center of which were the women and children, and the wounded. Purple troops were charging the west side of this square now, and smoke from many rifles curled upward in the still morning air.

Jimmy Christopher watched, with his heart beating fast, while those enemy horsemen charged right up to the defenders of the square, only to break at the last moment and fall back.

Involuntarily, Jimmy cheered. Storm's men had repulsed the enemy!

But how long could they last like this? Jimmy wondered why help was not forthcoming from the American lines. Willow Creek Pass was in sight from here, and the Americans there must surely see the fight going on below them. And then Jimmy snapped his fingers. Of course! Storm's men were in the Purple uniforms! The Americans might think that this was an internal fight going on among the Central Empire troops.

Colonel Smithfield should know about Storm's men, but then Colonel Smithfield might have been relieved, sent to some other position. This pass was a spot for infantry to defend, and not for cavalry.

Jimmy frowned, squinting against the sun, as he watched the enemy ranks reforming for another charge. This time they were forming on three sides of the square. They were going to charge simultaneously from all three directions! The square would surely break this time!

If only he could communicate with the Americans who were watching from the pass! If only he could make them understand that these were fellow Americans in need of help!

CHAPTER 8
SHERIDAN TO THE RESCUE

DESPERATELY, OPERATOR 5 cast about for some means of apprising the Americans at the pass that they must intervene. And abruptly, he snapped his fingers. His eyes sparkled. Swiftly his fingers delved into the inner pocket of his tunic, and removed from it a flat black case, which contained make-up material that he had expected to use in changing his appearance. He had discarded that original plan, and had forgotten entirely about the make-up case. Now he opened it eagerly; extracted a small mirror from it.

He dismounted, and knelt on the hard rock, in a spot where the bright morning sun shone brilliantly.

He experimented with the mirror, moving it from one position to another, until it caught the sun's rays, sent them slanting across the valley toward Willow Creek Pass. He held the mirror in his left hand, passing his right over it at short and long intervals, so that the flashes became dots and dashes of Morse Code. He flashed: *"Operator 5 calling! Operator 5 calling!"*

He kept repeating the call for almost three minutes. Three minutes can be a long time when one sees his friends surrounded by enemy troops hungry for their blood, about to launch an irresistible attack. Jimmy Christopher probably never spent a longer three minutes in his life until his eyes were gladdened by an answering flash from high up in Willow Creek Pass. Their heliograph was answering him!

"Identify yourself!"

With heart beating like a triphammer he paused a moment, glancing down into the valley. Bugles were blowing down there, and drums were beating.

The enemy was charging!

From three sides they came, close-packed cavalry that rode squarely into the hail of lead that Storm's riflemen hurled at them. The Purple armies always attacked in close formation. Rudolph never spared his own men, any more than he did an enemy's. Man-power was the cheapest thing that the Purple Emperor possessed, for he could draw upon the four corners of the earth for recruits. And though losses were heavier from the close-formation method of attack, results were more quickly attained—and it was results that Rudolph and Marshal Kremer wanted.

The thick ranks of the charging troopers were decimated by the fire of the riflemen. But there were, after all, only a hundred and seventy men under Storm, augmented by another fifty or sixty women who had weapons. That pitiably small company could not hope to hold off a regiment of cavalry, which was about what the enemy seemed to have in the field.

The riflemen were firing fast, and Jimmy could imagine their guns growing hot in their hands. The enemy ranks broke on two sides, and fell back a little, to re-form. On the third side, however, they reached the front rank of the square, and Operator 5 could see flashing sabers as they engaged in hand-to-hand conflict.

All this time he had been flashing his call signal. And now, as the answering heliograph came to him from the pass, he flashed back the code word that would prove to the officer in command there that he was really Operator 5: *"Bunker Hill!"*

At once the confirming flash came to him, then: *"Hank Sheridan standing by for message!"*

Jimmy frowned. If that was Hank Sheridan, why had he not gone to the rescue of the beleaguered riflemen? Surely Smithfield must have told Hank of the expedition of Storm's men. Hank should have guessed that these were the Wyoming riflemen returning. There was something queer here.

Nevertheless, he delivered his message, using the Morse Code. He knew Morse so well that he could send and receive messages without the necessity of transcribing them. And almost automatically, he flashed his news with the mirror. The Purple troops would also read that message, but it could not be helped. That was the trouble with the heliograph—it could not be kept secret. And even coded messages could be broken with a little application. That was why it had been necessary to send Tim and Diane with word-of-mouth instructions instead of trusting to heliograph or carrier-pigeons.

Now Jimmy flashed: *"Detachment now being attacked in valley are Storm's Northern Wyoming Riflemen, in enemy uniform. Go to their aid quickly for God's sake!"*

The answer came back instantaneously. *"Coming. I didn't know anything about them!"*

Jimmy put down his mirror, and watched the fight in the valley. Now he understood why Sheridan hadn't gone to Storm's assistance. Colonel Smithfield had told him nothing about the venture, for Sheridan had forbidden it. Hank had not even known that Storm's men were over the lines. He had no doubt suspected that this was some sort of ruse on the enemy's part, to draw the Americans out of the pass!

THE FIGHT was growing fiercer. One side of the square was broken now, and the enemy troops had pushed through into the center, overwhelming the riflemen by odds of four to one.

Groups of women fought desperately against the enemy troopers, defending the cots where their children and their wounded lay. The fight was bitter, merciless.

Operator 5 tore the major's uniform jacket off, slipped on his own tunic and cap, and spurred his horse down the ridge toward the fight. He reached the plain, and raced recklessly toward the broken square, pistol in hand.

There was nothing between him and the square of riflemen now, but another force of enemy cavalry came into sight at the north end of the valley, spurring fast toward the site of the battle. At the same time, Jimmy's heart was gladdened at the sight of a long column of American infantry debouching out of Willow Creek Pass. The Americans under Hank Sheridan were coming! The enemy must have read that heliograph message of Operator 5's, and they had thrown in a reserve regiment of cavalry. This promised to develop into a pitched battle! Jimmy Christopher was nearing the battle, while the American column advanced at the double-quick from the pass. The enemy reinforcements were coming up at Jimmy's right.

The first inkling of disaster that Jimmy Christopher had was the sight of the apparently riderless horse racing away from the enemy reinforcing regiment.

It had evidently been lashed to a frenzy, for it was racing with lathering mouth, directly at the column of American infantry. Jimmy gave it only a single glance, then spurred ahead, anxious to join the fight. But something—perhaps a telepathic instinct, caused him to throw a second glance in the direction of that horse. And now his eyes narrowed, and he felt a sudden surge of ungovernable rage. He recognized the chestnut hair of Diane Elliot, who was lashed to that horse! And alongside her was a shell, to which was attached a burning fuse!

Diane was strapped to the right side of the horse, her back against the shell, so that Jimmy had not sighted her at first. It took his breath away. That horse would plunge wildly into the ranks of the marching American infantry, and the fuse, already burning low, would ignite the powder in the shell. Diane would be blown to bits, together with several hundred American infantrymen!

The fiendish ingenuity of the idea caused Jimmy's fists to clench with rage. It was things like these, uncalled-for excesses of cruelty and murderous ingenuity, that had increased the hatred of the Americans for the enemy by a thousandfold.

Jimmy Christopher swerved his horse violently, spurred it forward to intercept Diane's wild steed. The Americans had also seen the shell and the lighted fuse; and they could have shot that horse down with ease. But they held their fire rather than blow up Diane Elliot with the shell.

Jimmy Christopher muttered: "Good boys!" They were taking a long chance on being blown to bits themselves, rather than deliberately bring about the death of Diane.

Operator 5 raced his horse to intercept the wild mount. The horse had evidently been maddened by bayonet stabs, but fortunately, it wore blinkers, which prevented its seeing Jimmy Christopher's approach. Thus, it did not swerve away when he reached its side, stretched out a hand and grasped its reins.

IT WAS a ticklish moment. If the horse A should kick free,

everything was lost. It would continue its wild dash for the American column. If Jimmy should take too long in subduing it, the fuse would burn down, and kill him as well as Diane.

Operator 5 used all the skill and knowledge of horses that he possessed. He kept a firm grip on the reins, riding beside the other horse, not dragging at it too much, and talking to it all the time in a soothing voice. At first the horse struggled, shying away from him. But after a moment it slowed, finally came to a panting stop!

Jimmy Christopher breathed a sigh of relief. There was sweat on his forehead. From the American ranks a cheer went up, and the column continued at the double quick, dividing into two sections. One section marched to the right toward the battle at the broken square, while the other swung to cut off the reinforcing cavalry.

Jimmy Christopher kept a careful hold on the reins of the riderless horse, while he dismounted. He snuffed out the fuse on the shell, and then cut Diane loose. She sighed, almost fainted, and then straightened up, forcing herself to retain consciousness.

"J-Jimmy!" she gasped. "T-that was a good job!"

Operator 5 took her in his arms. "Diane! How did you get in this mess?"

"They caught me about five miles from here. Kremer himself is with these troops. It was his idea to tie me to that shell. He said the Americans were too chivalrous to shoot a woman, even if she was bringing them a deadly shell."

"Thank God he was right!" Jimmy Christopher said.

The battle was almost over. The American column had driven

the enemy back from Captain Storm's square, with heavy losses; while the reinforcing cavalry, seeing themselves opposed by solid ranks of infantry, withdrew rather than risk a pitched battle.

Several hundred Purple prisoners were taken. Hank Sheridan rode over to where Jimmy and Diane were watching the mopping-up process. He shook hands with Jimmy.

"Damn it, Operator 5, you had express orders not to go on that mad venture. And you went anyway! No wonder Smithfield didn't dare to tell me about it!"

They moved back into the pass, resuming their previous position. "I don't think I'll try to hold that valley," Hank told Operator 5. "We're better off in the pass here."

Storm's riflemen were warmly congratulated by the other American troops, and the women and children were conducted to a field hospital safely behind the lines.

It was well on in the morning when Jimmy Christopher saw Hank Sheridan again. "Have you heard anything from Tim Donovan?" he asked.

Hank dropped his eyes. "Y-yes. I—I didn't want to tell you, before. It would have made you feel bad, and there isn't anything you could do about it—"

"Quick, Hank!" Jimmy gripped his arm hard. "What happened? Is—is he—killed?

"No. But it's almost as bad. We got a heliograph flash from one of our stations in the occupied territory, relayed through Colorado Springs. Tim Donovan was captured in Council Grove today!"

For a long moment Jimmy Christopher was silent. He knew

JIMMY CHRISTOPHER

that capture for Tim Donovan would mean death—just as it would for himself.

Hank Sheridan clapped a kindly hand on his shoulder. "Keep a stiff upper lip, Jimmy. I've flashed orders to our agents in Topeka to try to locate the kid—to find what the Emperor is going to do with him. When we find out where they've got the kid, maybe we can do something about it."

Diane Elliot was standing a few feet away. She came over; put her hand on Jimmy's arm. "I knew about it, too. Are you angry that we kept it from you?"

Numbly, Jimmy shook his head. "I've got to look for the kid," he said miserably. "I've got to go—"

"You can't!" Hank Sheridan said sharply. "You've got to be here for zero hour. You planned the campaign, and you have to be here to carry it out. You understand, Operator 5?"

Silently, Jimmy inclined his head. He knew that duty required his presence here. But his heart would be somewhere in the Occupied Territory with a little, freckle-faced Irish lad....

CHAPTER 9
PRISONER OF WAR

IN THE headquarters of the Purple armies at Topeka, Rudolph I, Emperor of the Central Empire, master of Europe and Asia, and self-styled Emperor of America, paced up and down the floor of the office which had once housed the governor of the State of Kansas, and which had been converted into a reception room for the emperor.

Rudolph at this time was no more than thirty-six years old, but the excesses which he permitted himself and the innate sadism of his nature had etched deep lines in his countenance, so that he looked like a man in his late forties.

This was the man who had ordered the massacre of Americans—without regard to sex or age—in every city in the Occupied Territory, on several occasions. This was the man who had devised new and fiendish methods of torture for those who defied the Imperial Edicts. This man was the man who had staged the crucifixion of a thousand civilians in order to amuse his guests at a gala ball. This was the man who had ordered American civilians buried to their necks in sand, and then trampled upon by a troop of cavalry. This was the man who had brought war, blood, rapine, torture and death to a peaceful America. And yet he was not satisfied. His narrow, sharp, blood-shot eyes hurled venom at the slim, wiry, freckle-faced Irish lad who stood before him, with hands bound behind his back.

Two huge troopers stood guard on either side of the boy, while Baron Julian Flexner, Prime Minister to His Imperial Majesty, stood a few feet away. Baron Flexner was tall, dapper, suave and shrewd. It was he who guided the foreign policy of the empire, he who smoothed over the horrible cruelties which his master perpetrated among conquered peoples. Here in America, Flexner had not found that task as easy as elsewhere. In Europe and Asia, he had been able to buy the allegiance of many people who had been severely wronged by the Emperor. Gold and the promise of high position had salved many a wound in the Old World. But in America, men had been strangely adamant to his bribes and his blandishments. He could not understand that Americans cherished liberty more than high-sounding titles and riches.

Only once had it been possible to influence Americans to aid and abet the Purple cause, and that instance had been one of severe stress, where the three Americans involved had thought that they were acting for the welfare of the country.*

Now he stared wonderingly at the stamina, the courage of this boy prisoner who was being cross-examined by the Emperor himself.

Rudolph had stepped up in front of the boy, and thrust his face close to the prisoner's.

"You do not deny that your name is Tim Donovan?" he rasped.

"No, sir. As long as Baron Flexner recognizes me, there's no use denying it."

Rudolph smiled dangerously. "You are the protégé of the man who is known as Operator 5. You were with him at Martinson's Farm when he and a troop of Americans disguised as loyal Imperial troopers attacked a company of my Uhlans. You were seen by the survivors, so you cannot deny that. After that, you left Operator 5, and you rode through the country for a day and a half, stopping at various places. Do you dare to deny those charges?"

Tim Donovan shrugged. "I admit nothing, and deny noth-

---

* AUTHOR'S NOTE: The incident referred to above was described in the novel entitled, "Patriots' Death Battalion." It refers to Redfern, Sinnott and Hartley, three American officers who became convinced after the death of the President of the United States that America's only salvation lay in surrender to the Purple Emperor. They accordingly attempted to put Operator 5 out of the way, considering that he was the only obstacle to surrender. They were not successful in their plan, and all three paid the extreme penalty.

ing. In other words, Your Imperial Highness—" his voice was controlled, but edged with scorn—"*I won't talk!*"

The boy thrust his jaw forward, so that it was within a half inch of Rudolph's.

The Emperor turned away, exclaimed: "Faugh! You, Flexner! You talk to this brat. Make him understand what will happen to him if he won't tell us what we want to know!"

Baron Flexner approached the lad with reluctance. Tim Donovan met the Prime Minister's gaze with a grin.

THESE TWO had met before, under very different circumstances. Only a few months before, the Baron's fourteen year-old daughter, Freda Flexner, had been made prisoner by Operator 5. Tim Donovan had come, disguised as a leper, to the Imperial Palace in New York, and had made a secret deal with Baron Flexner—the return of his daughter for the freedom of Operator 5's twin sister, Nan Christopher, who was at that time held prisoner, together with the ex-sergeant of Royal Canadian Police, Aloysius MacTavish. Flexner had agreed, and had surreptitiously aided Tim to arrange the escape of Nan Christopher and Sergeant MacTavish. A week later, Tim Donovan had escorted Freda Flexner, through the enemy lines, back to her father.*

---

* AUTHOR'S NOTE: The incident above referred to was related in the novel entitled, "Revolt of the Lost Legions." To a good many of our readers, who have not had access to the hitherto unpublished notes of Operator 5 regarding the Purple Invasion, this incident was news. Until recently it had always been a matter of speculation as to how Nan Christopher and Sergeant MacTavish had managed to effect their escape from the under-

Now, as Flexner looked at the boy, it was very evident that the Prime Minister was extremely embarrassed. There were two reasons for this embarrassment, but neither of those reasons was known to the Emperor. In the first place, Flexner was in a cold sweat lest Tim should be tortured and in his agony reveal the fact that Flexner had aided in the escape of Nan Christopher; and the second reason was that his daughter, Freda, had developed a strong friendship for this freckle-faced boy during the period of her captivity. And though Freda was only fourteen years old, Flexner stood a good deal in awe of her tongue. He was himself a widower, and he had become more and more used to the companionship of his daughter. He knew of her fondness for Tim Donovan, and had refrained from informing her

ground dungeon of the Imperial Palace where they had been confined pending the execution of the sentence of crucifixion upon them. Since the publication of the inside story of this incident last month, many historians will have to revise their theories concerning the matter. Even so careful a historian as Harrison Stievers has been forced to go to the realms of fancy for an explanation; in chapter nineteen of his monumental work on the Purple Invasion, he hints that Nan Christopher stabbed a guard who entered her cell to attack her, and that she then took the guard's keys and opened the cell of Sergeant MacTavish. This is manifestly untrue, for the personal diary of Emperor Rudolph for that day shows that the guard was found *shot* to death, and not *stabbed*—which coincides with the version of the story here related, as found in the memoirs of Operator 5. To all those of our readers who have written to congratulate us upon revealing this bit of hidden history, we extend our heartiest thanks. *C. S.*

that he lad had been captured at a secret meeting of civilians in the cellar of a house at Council Grove, only a few hours before. He feared what she would say if she learned that Tim had been executed without her father's attempting to save him.

So now, he approached the boy perplexedly, not knowing just how to handle him. If Rudolph detected the least hint of leniency in his attitude, the Emperor would be likely to dismiss him and handle the matter personally—in which case, Tim Donovan's fate would be sealed and mere punishment of death fortunate.

"Look here, my boy," he said gruffly. "You are very foolish not to talk. We know that you were in Council Grove for the purpose of giving the American civilians there a date for rising to co-operate with the American Defense Force. We merely want to know what that date is. Unfortunately, the raid took place before you were able to impart the information to the others, or else we should have been able to drag it from them by torture. Now why don't you give us the information, and save yourself a lot of agony?"

Tim Donovan grinned at him. *"I'm not talking, Herr Baron!"* he said.

Flexner breathed a sigh of relief. He understood by the emphasis Tim had placed on the words; that the boy meant that he would not betray Flexner's former action in aiding the escape of Nan Christopher. But he also knew that few people could resist the exquisite tortures which Rudolph's pet executioners used. The boy might intend to shield him....

TIM HAD been captured by an unfortunate accident. He had

Freda came running
from the tent.

practically completed his mission after leaving Jimmy Christopher and the Wyoming riflemen at the Martinson Farm. He had ridden east and had contacted all of the local leaders except for Samuel Pinkerton at Council Grove. This was his last rendezvous, and he kept it at the appointed time. Unfortunately, the Purple Espionage system had already established surveillance over Samuel Pinkerton, and the cellar of Pinkerton's home was raided just as the meeting began. After a fight, Tim Donovan was captured.

Now, Baron Flexner attempted to cajole the lad into talking, using all the power of his suave eloquence. But to everything he said Tim Donovan maintained a stoical silence. Rudolph kept pacing the floor during the inquisition, growing more and more impatient.

At last he burst out irritably: "For God's sake, Flexner, have done with this. Send the brat downstairs. Have his thumbs twisted out of their sockets, and then question him again. He'll talk, all right. I want to know more than the date of that uprising. I want to know where to find Operator 5. He knows. And by God, he'll tell!" *

Flexner moved to obey.

Tim Donovan stood quietly between his two burly guards, without uttering a word. He knew that there was absolutely nothing in the make-up of Rudolph to prevent him from carry-

---

* AUTHOR'S NOTE: Rudolph's anxiety to find Operator 5 will be easily understood by those who have followed the history of the Purple War. It will be recalled that from the very first days of the invasion, it was Operator 5 who opposed the onward, cross-continent sweep of the bloody empire, who slowed up and often stopped the advance of the Purple Armies, and who defied the Emperor at every turn. It was Operator 5 who made the Purple Empire the laughingstock of the whole world by capturing a first-class Purple Battleship from right under the noses of the entire fleet. For this, and for various other exploits, Rudolph entertained a deep, bitter hatred for Operator 5. And he had gone so far as to offer a fabulous reward for his capture, dead or alive—that reward being the governorship of an entire province in the Occupied Territory for the man who captured him!

ing out his threat. Tim felt an empty sensation at the pit of his stomach at the thought of having his thumbs twisted from his sockets. In New York a few months ago, he had seen a deserter from the Purple Army who had been treated in that manner.

The man's hands were a gruesome, repelling sight. And in the man's eyes there had still been the reflection of the unbearable agony he had endured. Tearing skin and flesh, crackling bones, ripping tendons and muscles—that was the ordeal to which Tim Donovan could look forward. Each time that the victim fainted, they relaxed the pressure of the vises, and waited until he recovered. Sometimes the process took as long as forty-eight hours, during which the searing agony of straining tendons burned into the very soul of a man. Tim Donovan was but a boy. Yet he stood rigid, refusing to speak; for he knew that if he betrayed Operator 5, that if Operator 5 were made a prisoner, the things that would be done to him would be ten thousand times worse.

Tim set his teeth, and shook his head when Flexner approached him, appealingly. "Won't you talk, boy, before you're taken away? It's your last chance!"

Rudolph laughed harshly. "You'll talk, brat! You'll come to me, crawling on your knees, and begging to talk! Take him away!"

Flexner was chewing his lip in desperate perplexity. If the boy broke down, he might babble of Flexner's complicity in Nan's escape. Rudolph's wrath would be terrible. The Prime Minister's mind worked swiftly, and suddenly he thought of a brilliant idea.

"Wait, Your Imperial Majesty!" he exclaimed. "I have just thought of something better!"

Rudolph looked at him curiously, a little impatiently. "Well? What is it, Flexner?"

The Baron stepped close to the Emperor. "If I may tell it to Your Imperial Majesty in private?"

Rudolph nodded, crossed the room toward the window, with Flexner close behind him.

TIM DONOVAN watched them with narrowed eyes. What was Flexner planning now? The wily Prime Minister could spin dangerous webs when he wanted to. Tim bit his lip in vexation. If he had only been more careful before entering the cellar of Samuel Pinkerton at Council Grove!

He did not care about himself. The torture would be terrible, of course, but he would endure it. He did not trust himself, however. He had heard of men going mad under the torture, of losing control of themselves, and of babbling out the truth without knowing it. If he should do that, he would never be able to forgive himself.

It would be so easy to say: "Zero hour is tomorrow at six-thirty! And those captured dispatches are false. The Americans are planning to attack at Berthoud Pass, and not at Concha. If you watch the lines around Willow Creek Pass, you'll catch Operator 5 tonight!"

The words dinned a steady symphony in Tim Donovan's mind, and he tried to push them away, to forget them. They must not remain in his consciousness when he went under the torture. His mind must be a blank. Oh God, if he could only make his mind a blank!

He became aware that Flexner had crossed the room, and

was standing in front of him once more. Rudolph had left the room through a side door.

"We have changed our plans," Flexner informed him. "You will not be tortured. Instead, you will be shot at sunrise tomorrow!"

Tim stared at him incredulously. Flexner had accomplished the impossible—had secured for him the favor of a quick death! But how? Why? What was behind this sudden leniency? What argument had he advance to Rudolph to make the emperor relent, to give up the chance of forcing information from the boy?

Tim said slowly: "I suppose I ought to thank you for the favor, Baron Flexner. But I'm afraid you have something up your sleeve."

Flexner shrugged. "If you decide to talk before morning, send one of the guards for me." He motioned to the two troopers, and they escorted Tim from the room. Tim wore a worried frown. He was puzzled at the sudden commutation of his punishment. He would have been even more worried had he seen what Flexner was doing in the room he had just left.

The Baron had rung a bell, summoning his aide-de-camp.

"Arrange to have a notice rushed through the printers!" he instructed curtly. "It is to be posted on every public building in the Occupied Territories of Kansas, Colorado and Nebraska. Also, print ten thousand additional copies, and send them over the American lines in toy balloons."

The secretary saluted. "It shall be done, *Herr* Baron. And the message is to be what?"

"Is to read thus," he dictated rapidly.

"To Operator 5: Your protégé, the Donovan boy, is to be shot at sunrise. There is only one way to save him—by supplying yourself as a substitute in the boy's place before the firing squad. I will guarantee you a quick death before the same firing squad. Remember, you have only till sunrise. The place of execution will be outside the city limits of Topeka, on the parade grounds. I am sure that a gallant man like yourself will not allow this boy to die in your place."

He gestured rapidly. "Then the signature, Baron Julian Flexner."

The secretary smiled cunningly as he wrote to the Baron's dictation. When he finished, he glanced up. "Permit me to say, *Herr* Baron, that this is a very clever scheme. The man must give himself up, or forever be branded a coward!"

Flexner nodded. "Yes, I must say that it is clever. It—er—takes care of several difficulties." His voice grew crisp. "Hurry. I want those notices printed and ready for distribution within one hour!"

Baron Julian Flexner, Prime Minister to His Imperial Majesty, Rudolph I stroked his moustache in smug satisfaction as the secretary hurried out. A smile of gratification wreathed his lips....

CHAPTER 10
A BULLET FOR THE EMPEROR

THAT TUESDAY night, Berthoud Pass and all the area behind it was a beehive of activity. American columns were converging on this spot from every point in the west, moving through the darkness without lights.

Five fast scout planes, conserving their precious store of fuel as much as possible, kept constantly in the air, to prevent enemy observers from coming over and spotting the concentration of troops at Berthoud.

Word had come through from American agents that the enemy reserves were still at Pueblo—which meant that Jimmy's false dispatches had reached Imperial Headquarters. The next day would be a nervous one, for the American troops would have to lie hidden all through the daylight hours, waiting for six-thirty.

Operator 5 was a dynamo of energy, issuing order after order, carrying in his head information about every American regiment, its exact location, its equipment, its numbers. He was trying to forget in a rush of work the fact that Tim Donovan was a prisoner somewhere behind the enemy lines. That evening, small black balloons had come floating over the lines, and numbers of them had dropped in camp.

Operator 5 had been curious about those messages, and he had asked Diane to go and get one. She had been away an unconscionably long time, and when she returned she did not have even one copy.

In reply to Jimmy Christopher's question, she replied carelessly: "Oh, it was just a manifesto demanding that we surrender. They threaten dreadful reprisals once they drive us back from the Continental Divide."

Jimmy Christopher shrugged. "They can't do worse than they've already done, Di." His face was drawn, strained, and there were dark rings under his eyes. Jimmy Christopher was working on the last of his physical resources, drawing upon every ounce of reserve energy in his powerful body. In addition, he had always, every minute of the night, to fight away the spectre of Tim Donovan as a prisoner.

"There should be some news of Tim," he said fretfully. "They know how attached I am to him. Knowing Rudolph as well as I do, I'd expect him to send me some sort of ultimatum—"

He broke off as Diane uttered a choked gasp, covered her face with her hands.

"Poor kid," he said softly. "You feel it as bad as I do. Why don't you go and get some rest?"

She raised her head, and he saw that her eyes were wet with tears.

"I—I think I will, Jimmy."

She left him, went into the tent of Hank Sheridan. She pulled the flap down behind her, and ran to him, letting herself go in a burst of tears.

"Oh, Hank," she sobbed, "it's dreadful, keeping that message from him. He—he just told me he was expecting some sort of ultimatum. And we have it here, and we're not telling him. He'll never forgive me!"

HANK SHERIDAN'S kindly old eyes were clouded as he got up and put a comforting arm around her shoulder. "It's the only thing we can do, Diane. If we told Jimmy what that message really contains, he'd go right away and give himself up to save Tim's life. And America needs him. America is greater than Tim, Diane. And I'm sure the boy wouldn't want to live at the expense of Jimmy's life!"

"I know, I know," Diane sobbed, "but it's such a cruel thing to do!" She was fingering the printed message, the ink of which was still fresh, which she had taken from the bosom of her blouse.

It was the notice which Baron Flexner had caused to be printed, notifying Operator 5 of the impending execution of Tim Donovan at dawn.

"I—I feel that I'm murdering Tim. I've *got* to tell Jimmy, Hank."

She broke off at the sound of clattering hooves outside. The flap was jerked back, and a dust-grimed American cavalryman leaped inside. He was panting from his hard ride, and he blurted out his message:

"General Sheridan! Compliments of Colonel Houston, commanding the heliograph station. A carrier pigeon has just arrived with a message from behind the enemy lines, from one of our agents. It states that Emperor Rudolph is himself at the front. He is inspecting the troops in Russel Gulch at this very moment!"

As the man made his report, Operator 5 had appeared in the tent opening behind him. Jimmy gripped the man's arm. "Repeat that!"

The cavalryman repeated the message. Jimmy Christopher's eyes were shining. "We've got to go after him! It's our big chance! If we could only get through the enemy lines and seize the Emperor—"

"Excuse me, sir," the cavalryman broke in. "If you want to get through, I know a way. It could only be used by a small force—"

"A small force is all we need. Quick, man, what is the way?"

"Well, sir, you remember the old Moffat Tunnel under the Continental Divide, for railroad trains? The old Denver and Rio Grande Western Railroad used to run through there. Well, the Purple troops destroyed the tunnel with dynamite, but I was poking around in there the other day, and there's a narrow passage that a man and horse could get through—if he wanted to take a chance on the whole mountain caving in on top of him."

"Of course I'll take a chance!" Operator 5 exclaimed. "And I'll want a hundred volunteers."

The cavalryman said eagerly: "Can I go, sir? I'm Smith, from Captain Storm's Wyoming Riflemen. I was with you yesterday at Martinson's farm. I'm sure the boys'll want to go. Shall I ask them?"

"Yes. Go ahead, Smith. And if you get a hundred volunteers, have them saddled and ready to ride in ten minutes!"

Smith saluted and left, and Jimmy Christopher faced Hank Sheridan. "Don't try to stop me, Hank," he said tightly. "You don't know what this means. If we capture Rudolph, the whole Purple campaign will crash!"

Hank Sheridan didn't smile. He said: "I won't try to stop you,

118

Jimmy." And then he turned to Diane, said cryptically: "You see what I meant when I said America needs him?"

THREE QUARTERS of an hour later, Operator 5, at the head of one hundred picked men from Storm's Wyoming Riflemen, rode along a dark side road that led directly into Russel Gulch. Their horses' hooves were bound with old rags to deaden the sound, and every man was careful that no metal should strike against metal to give off the faintest sound. The agent who had sent the message by carrier pigeon was waiting just where the road debouched into the gulch.

"There they are sir," he reported. "Rudolph has a guard of two hundred Imperial Lancers. They're just mounting to ride. Rudolph is going south to inspect the troops around Concha Pass."

Jimmy Christopher nodded. "You've done a good night's work, Chisholm, whether we get him or not. America is deeply in your debt."

"Thank you, sir. But I'm afraid you're going to have your hands full, Operator 5. The Imperial Lancers outnumber you two to one—"

Storm, who was riding beside Operator 5, laughed harshly. "We're used to odds like that, Chisholm. Let's go, Operator 5!"

Jimmy nodded, raised his arm. The troops surged forward, spurring their mounts ahead.

In the darkness they could see the close-grouped troop of Imperial Lancers, with their tall shakos and long swords, held at salute. Rudolph I, Emperor of the Purple Empire, was mounting his horse, assisted by an orderly.

The Wyoming troops charged—but Rudolph,
snarling with rage, was mounting to flee.

Now the galloping troop of riflemen were within a hundred feet of the lancers. Someone spotted them, raised the alarm. A bugle sounded, and guttural voices issued swift orders to the lancers, who quickly formed a square around their emperor.

Jimmy Christopher shouted in a stentorian voice: "At the double-quick—*charge!*"

The riflemen thundered behind him, forming a wedge of which he was the apex. Straight for the center of that square of Imperial Lancers they charged, and the lancers broke before them. Nothing could withstand the impact of these American horsemen.

Jimmy Christopher's saber flashed like a spitting cobra in the night, driving to the right, to the left, slashing, and parrying; but he continually urged his horse forward toward the spot where the regally attired figure of Rudolph was scrambling onto his horse.

Rudolph got into the saddle, and looked behind; saw Operator 5 driving at him. His face became contorted into a snarl of rage, but he did not wait to fight. Instead he spurred his horse away, bending low.

Operator 5 made to follow him, but found his way barred by a dozen lancers. Jimmy Christopher fought like a madman, watching the fleeing Rudolph out of the corner of his eye. Rudolph was far down the gulch now, while the battle raged here. Operator 5 slashed a wide circle around himself with his saber, and drew his revolver. He raised it, fired a single shot after the fleeing Emperor. He saw Rudolph sway in his saddle, but he did not fall. The emperor's horse with its rider disappeared into the night.

BITTERLY JIMMY CHRISTOPHER fought on. He had failed. He knew he had wounded the emperor, but he could not tell whether it was a mortal wound. Now the two hundred lancers—or those who remained of them—fought without spirit. The Americans drove them backward along the gulch, until, with one impulse, they turned and fled.

Operator 5 blew a single blast on his whistle to recall the riflemen from the pursuit. "It's no use, boys," he said. "We could never follow Rudolph in the darkness. He's escaped for now. Let's get back."

He led a dejected troop back toward the Moffat Tunnel. None of them had really expected to succeed in capturing the emperor. But they had been so close to it, that to fail was bitter.

Captain Storm placed a consoling hand on Jimmy's arm. "Cheer up, Operator 5. You hit him, anyway. Maybe you got him in a vital spot—"

He broke off at the abrupt drumming of a horse's hooves in the night. Almost at once, they heard other horses, behind the first. Someone was being pursued!

Hurriedly, Jimmy Christopher disposed his men on both sides of the road, enjoined silence.

In a moment, two riders came into sight. Behind them a troop of Uhlans were strung out in irregular order. They were closing in on the fugitives, and now they began to fire at them. One was a boy, the other a girl, but this girl was no tattered and ragged refugee.

Her horse, too, was thoroughbred, a sorrel that still spurned the earth lightly, outdistancing the cavalry mounts of the Purple troopers despite a wound that pumped blood with every stride of the swelling haunch muscles. On the girl's breast gleamed a golden order of the Purple Empire, and yet—with a white and agonized face narrowed her slender shoulders against the whistling lead that the Purple troopers were aiming at a woman of their own nation!

Operator 5 leaped into the road. His eyes narrowed, for on the other thoroughbred horse that tore along beside the girl's, in the freckled hand stretched to the rein to drag along the wounded horse still faster, in the freckled face that encouraged the girl, Operator 5 recognized Tim Donovan!

"Tim!" he shouted. And to the Wyoming riflemen: "Right and left deploy! Extend flanks as skirmishers! With full clips, load! For volley fire by platoons—load—aim—"

The maneuver was like lightning. The line of men who had been facing the road, prepared to capture a horseman, were now at right angles to it, and fifty repeating rifles covered the charging Uhlans. Still Tim and the girl masked the fire. Operator 5 waited—waited till they thundered past him, while the Uhlans' bullets sang in his ears. They were by—and the alert Tim had snatched the girl from her saddle, swung from his horse, and jumped into cover.

"Fire!" shouted Operator 5. In one crashing thunder-roll fifty rifles belched flame, steel, and death. Like two invisible scythes that volley swept the road, bullets from the right and left platoons merging in a murderous cross-fire. A machine gun

124

could have swept the road no more effectively, and not even a machine gun could have blasted the whole front of the Purple cavalry with five successive deluges of lead that followed each other as swift as bolts could be slid home and triggers pulled.

The front of the Purple troop collapsed in a heap of riddled men and kicking blood-dappled horses. Those in the rear could not check themselves. On they came, a few men, screaming in terror of certain destruction.

The Wyoming Riflemen needed no orders now. They popped out from their places of concealment. Their swords flashed in the night, their guns barked a merciless message of death as the pursuing Uhlans were cut down to the last man.

Operator 5 did not join the fight. He was shaking hands almost hysterically with Tim Donovan and with the girl.

"You know Freda Flexner, don't you, Jimmy?" Tim said.

Jimmy nodded. "But how did you get here? I heard you were a prisoner—"

"Right. I was to be shot at sunrise, but Rudolph decided he couldn't wait. He ordered me shot at once. They had my grave dug, and the firing squad lined up, and then Freda here came running out of one of the tents. She had heard I was to be shot, and she wouldn't stand for it. She pointed a gun at the officer in command of the firing squad, and he was a little worried about shooting Baron Flexner's daughter. So we backed out of there, and Freda had horses ready. The Uhlans chased us, and here we are!"

Jimmy Christopher's eyes were suspiciously moist as he

hugged Freda Flexner. "You're a brick, Freda. When we drive your armies out of here, we'll erect a statue to you!"

TIM DONOVAN immediately became serious. "That reminds me, Jimmy. I've got some bad news for you."

He produced a folded poster, which he handed to him. "Freda brought that along. She thought it might interest you to have the news in advance. It's to be posted in every city hall in the country tomorrow."

Operator 5 felt strange misgivings as he unfolded the poster. Those misgivings were verified as he read:

IMPERIAL HEADQUARTERS PURPLE EMPIRE IN AMERICA

BE IT KNOWN:

That if the American Defense Force does not withdraw from the Continental Divide on or before Wednesday, June 30th, of this, the Fifth Year of the Purple Empire, we shall visit the following punishment upon every family resident in the Occupied Territory,

NAMELY: That the eldest son in each family will be forthwith taken from his home and shot to death!

No appeal shall be taken from this edict, and no exceptions shall be made.

Signed,
Rudolph, Rex-Imperator.

Operator 5's lips were a thin, tight line. Captain Storm, who had read the message over his shoulder, said: "Good God! The men won't fight if it means the death of their oldest sons."

"They'll fight!" Operator 5 said grimly. "Rudolph doesn't know Americans."

"What can we do to stop that slaughter?" Storm demanded. "Think of it—"

"I'm thinking of it. And we'll find some way to stop it. They can't lick us with a threat like that!"

The small cavalcade rode grimly, silently, back toward the Moffat Tunnel. They were carrying with them news that was to be vital to the future of America.*

---

* AUTHOR'S NOTE: How America met the threat embodied in that procla-mation of Rudolph's will be related in the next novel. In connection with that threat, Operator 5 was compelled with his small band of devoted friends, to undertake the most grueling task that any man has ever been called upon to face. The unquenchable flame of freedom that burned in one man's soul lit a conflagration that spread from coast to coast.

POPULAR HERO PULPS AVAILABLE NOW:

THE SPIDER

❑ #1: The Spider Strikes	$13.95
❑ #2: The Wheel of Death	$13.95
❑ #3: Wings of the Black Death	$13.95
❑ #4: City of Flaming Shadows	$13.95
❑ #5: Empire of Doom!	$13.95
❑ #6: Citadel of Hell	$13.95
❑ #7: The Serpent of Destruction	$13.95
❑ #8: The Mad Horde	$13.95
❑ #9: Satan's Death Blast	$13.95
❑ #10: The Corpse Cargo	$13.95
❑ #11: Prince of the Red Looters	$13.95
❑ #12: Reign of the Silver Terror	$13.95
❑ #13: Builders of the Dark Empire	$13.95
❑ #14: Death's Crimson Juggernaut	$13.95
❑ #15: The Red Death Rain	$13.95
❑ #16: The City Destroyer	$13.95
❑ #17: The Pain Emperor	$13.95
❑ #18: The Flame Master	$13.95
❑ #19: Slaves of the Crime Master	$13.95
❑ #20: Reign of the Death Fiddler	$13.95
❑ #21: Hordes of the Red Butcher	$13.95
❑ #22: Dragon Lord of the Underworld	$13.95
❑ #23: Master of the Death-Madness	$13.95
❑ #24: King of the Red Killers	$13.95
❑ #25: Overlord of the Damned	$13.95
❑ #26: Death Reign of the Vampire King	$13.95
❑ #27: Emperor of the Yellow Death	$13.95
❑ #28: The Mayor of Hell	$13.95
❑ #29: Slaves of the Murder Syndicate	$13.95
❑ #30: Green Globes of Death	$13.95
❑ #31: The Cholera King	$13.95
❑ #32: Slaves of the Dragon	$13.95
❑ #33: Legions of Madness	$12.95
❑ #34: Laboratory of the Damned	$12.95
❑ #35: Satan's Sightless Legion	$12.95
❑ #36: The Coming of the Terror	$12.95
❑ #37: The Devil's Death-Dwarfs	$12.95
❑ #38: City of Dreadful Night	$12.95
❑ #39: Reign of the Snake Men	$12.95
❑ #40: Dictator of the Damned	$12.95
❑ #41: The Mill-Town Massacres	$12.95
❑ #42: Satan's Workshop	$12.95

❑ #43: Scourge of the Yellow Fangs	$12.95
❑ #44: The Devil's Pawnbroker	$12.95
❑ #45: Voyage of the Coffin Ship	$12.95
❑ #46: The Man Who Ruled in Hell	$13.95
❑ #47: Slaves of the Black Monarch	$13.95
❑ #48: Machineguns Over the White House	$13.95
❑ #49: The City That Dared Not Eat	$13.95
❑ #50: Master of the Flaming Horde	$13.95
❑ #51: Satan's Switchboard	$13.95
❑ #52: Legions of the Accursed Light	$13.95
❑ #53: The City of Lost Men	$13.95
❑ #54: The Grey Horde Creeps	$13.95
❑ #55: City of Whispering Death	$13.95
❑ #56: When Thousands Slept in Hell	$13.95
❑ #57: Satan's Shakles	$14.95
❑ #58: The Emperor From Hell	$14.95
❑ #59: The Devil's Candlesticks	$14.95
❑ #60: The City That Paid to Die	$14.95
❑ *NEW:* #61: The Spider at Bay	$14.95

THE WESTERN RAIDER

❑ #1: Guns of the Damned	$13.95
❑ #2: The Hawk Rides Back from Death	$13.95
❑ #3: Gun-Call for the Lost Legion	$13.95
❑ #4: The Law of Silver Trent	$13.95
❑ #5: The Gun-Prayer of Silver Trent	$13.95
❑ #6: Silver Trent Rides Alone	$13.95

G-8 AND HIS BATTLE ACES

❑ #1: The Bat Staffel	$13.95

CAPTAIN SATAN

❑ #1: The Mask of the Damned	$13.95
❑ #2: Parole for the Dead	$13.95
❑ #3: The Dead Man Express	$13.95
❑ #4: A Ghost Rides the Dawn	$13.95
❑ #5: The Ambassador From Hell	$13.95

DR. YEN SIN

❑ #1: Mystery of the Dragon's Shadow	$12.95
❑ #2: Mystery of the Golden Skull	$12.95
❑ #3: Mystery of the Singing Mummies	$12.95

POPULAR HERO PULPS AVAILABLE NOW:

ACE G-MAN
- ❏ #1: The Suicide Squad Reports for Death $14.95
- ❏ #2: Coffins for the Suicide Squad $14.95

OPERATOR 5
- ❏ #1: The Masked Invasion $13.95
- ❏ #2: The Invisible Empire $13.95
- ❏ #3: The Yellow Scourge $13.95
- ❏ #4: The Melting Death $13.95
- ❏ #5: Cavern of the Damned $13.95
- ❏ #6: Master of Broken Men $13.95
- ❏ #7: Invasion of the Dark Legions $13.95
- ❏ #8: The Green Death Mists $13.95
- ❏ #9: Legions of Starvation $13.95
- ❏ #10: The Red Invader $13.95
- ❏ #11: The League of War-Monsters $13.95
- ❏ #12: The Army of the Dead $13.95
- ❏ #13: March of the Flame Marauders $13.95
- ❏ #14: Blood Reign of the Dictator $13.95
- ❏ #15: Invasion of the Yellow Warlords $13.95
- ❏ #16: Legions of the Death Master $13.95
- ❏ #17: Hosts of the Flaming Death $13.95
- ❏ #18: Invasion of the Crimson Death Cult $13.95
- ❏ #19: Attack of the Blizzard Men $13.95
- ❏ #20: Scourge of the Invisible Death $13.95
- ❏ #21: Raiders of the Red Death $13.95
- ❏ #22: War-Dogs of the Green Destroyer $13.95
- ❏ #23: Rockets From Hell $13.95
- ❏ #24: War-Masters from the Orient $13.95
- ❏ #25: Crime's Reign of Terror $13.95
- ❏ #26: Death's Ragged Army $13.95
- ❏ #27: Patriots' Death Battalion $13.95
- ❏ #28: The Bloody Forty-five Days $13.95
- ❏ #29: America's Plague Battalions $13.95
- ❏ #30: Liberty's Suicide Legions $13.95
- ❏ #31: Siege of the Thousand Patriots $13.95
- ❏ #32: Patriots' Death March $14.95
- ❏ #33: Revolt of the Lost Legions $14.95
- ❏ **NEW:** #34: Drums of Destruction $14.95

CAPTAIN COMBAT
- ❏ #1: The Sky Beast of Berlin $13.95
- ❏ #2: Red Wings For the Blood Battalion $13.95
- ❏ #3: Low Ceiling For Nazi Hell Hawks $13.95

DUSTY AYRES AND HIS BATTLE BIRDS
- ❏ #1: Black Lightning! $13.95
- ❏ #2: Crimson Doom $13.95
- ❏ #3: The Purple Tornado $13.95
- ❏ #4: The Screaming Eye $13.95
- ❏ #5: The Green Thunderbolt $13.95
- ❏ #6: The Red Destroyer $13.95
- ❏ #7: The White Death $13.95
- ❏ #8: The Black Avenger $13.95
- ❏ #9: The Silver Typhoon $13.95
- ❏ #10: The Troposphere F-S $13.95
- ❏ #11: The Blue Cyclone $13.95
- ❏ #12: The Tesla Raiders $13.95

MAVERICKS
- ❏ #1: Five Against the Law $12.95
- ❏ #2: Mesquite Manhunters $12.95
- ❏ #3: Bait for the Lobo Pack $12.95
- ❏ #4: Doc Grimson's Outlaw Posse $12.95
- ❏ #5: Charlie Parr's Gunsmoke Cure $12.95

THE MYSTERIOUS WU FANG
- ❏ #1: The Case of the Six Coffins $12.95
- ❏ #2: The Case of the Scarlet Feather $12.95
- ❏ #3: The Case of the Yellow Mask $12.95
- ❏ #4: The Case of the Suicide Tomb $12.95
- ❏ #5: The Case of the Green Death $12.95
- ❏ #6: The Case of the Black Lotus $12.95
- ❏ #7: The Case of the Hidden Scourge $12.95

THE SECRET 6
- ❏ #1: The Red Shadow $13.95
- ❏ #2: House of Walking Corpses $13.95
- ❏ #3: The Monster Murders $13.95
- ❏ #4: The Golden Alligator $13.95

CAPTAIN ZERO
- ❏ #1: City of Deadly Sleep $13.95
- ❏ #2: The Mark of Zero! $13.95
- ❏ #3: The Golden Murder Syndicate $13.95